Hurricane Beach

A Sweet Second-Chance Romance - Large Print Edition

Southern Storms

Book 1

Lexie Nicholas

Hurricane Beach
By Lexie Nicholas

* * *

Edited by Kat Nics
Cover Design by Nickie Cochran

Chapter 1

Heat lightning painted the southern night sky in the distance as Anna spotted a sign for the I-95 exit. Her body relaxed, and a sigh of relief escaped her. After four endless and grueling days on the road, they were close now. In less than half an hour, they would arrive in Magnolia Hill. Home.

It'd been too long.

"You're moving to the country?" her medic colleagues at the fire station had asked her on her last day of work as a paramedic.

"Why wouldn't I?" she had countered, as if it was the most absurd question of all. "I grew up there. It's not as bad as you think."

Her friends couldn't understand why, out of all places, she would trade the mountains of Colorado to move to Georgia. Yes, Magnolia Hill was in the boonies. Yes, the only two seasons in Southeast Georgia ranged from hot to not-so-hot. Even so, she knew she had made the right decision. She craved the comfort of home. Anna needed the people she loved most in her life, especially now. To be honest, she was lucky to still be alive.

Yes, home was where she needed to be to heal.

She glanced over at her daughter, Ashleigh, who was fast asleep, when the engine began to sputter and the moving truck lost speed. She punched the gas pedal to the metal, but the truck only continued to slow. "No! No! No!!!"

Ashleigh woke up. "What? Are we at Grandma's yet?" she asked, mumbling her words and rubbing her eyes.

"I wish, sweetie. The truck broke down." Judging by Ashleigh's exasperated sigh, she wasn't all too happy about it, either. It'd been a long drive, and both of them were sick of traveling.

Anna dug through the glove compartment for the customer service number on the truck's paperwork. "We'll have someone there in about an hour," the lady told her when she called. An hour.

Ashleigh didn't seem to care, not that she cared about any aspect of the move. She reshaped her pillow and placed it against the window to go back to sleep, earbuds in and her phone in her lap.

Anna was fully aware that the teen's silent treatment was only a hint at how mad her daughter was. She couldn't blame her for her anger. She had ripped her away from her skater friends, her school, and all that was familiar to her. Anna sighed. Someday, Ashleigh would understand why they had to move, even if she hated her for it now. She'd come around eventually.

She shoved the rental truck paperwork back into the glove compartment, then dialed Maggie's number. Knowing her, she was already waiting restlessly for them to pull up any moment now. "Mom," Anna said. "Bad news. The truck died on us, and the road service will be at least another hour before they can get out here. Why don't you go to bed? It'll probably be late by the time we roll up."

"Not a chance. I'll be bright-eyed and bushy-tailed, even if you get here after midnight. This ole' lady still has some life left in her."

"Okay, Mom." She knew better than to argue with her. "I have to warn you, though. It might take a while. I'll call you when we're back on the road."

"That's fine, darlin'. Just promise to be safe."

"I will, Mom."

They ended the call, and all she could do now was wait. Anna leaned back into her seat and watched the lightning zigzag across the eastern horizon, revealing for a split second the ominous thunderheads towering off the coast. What she wouldn't give to be a teenager again. She remembered the thrill of chasing after storms with her friends. They thought they were invincible then. Those were the good times. Maybe once she started working again and making ends meet, she'd have time to reconnect with them.

She yawned and closed her eyes. There was nothing wrong with a quick shut-eye until road service arrived.

Bright orange flashing lights ripped Anna out of her semi-conscious state. She blinked. In her rearview mirror, she noticed a utility truck pulling up behind her. A man wearing a neon yellow safety vest and a ball cap walked up to her door.

This must be the roadside service and not a serial killer disguised as a tow truck driver, she told herself. Darn horror movies.

She rolled down her window only a few inches, just in case.

"Mrs. Weaver?" he asked.

She crossed herself and sent a silent thank you upward. It was Ms. Weaver now, but she was too tired to bother correcting him.

"So you're broke down?" he asked.

"I am," she replied. "We were so close to home, too!"

"Where's home, if you don't mind me asking?"

"Magnolia Hill."

"Oh, yeah? That is close." He nodded toward the front of the truck. "Well, ma'am, if you pop the hood, I'll try to get you back on the road in no time."

Thirty minutes later, the mechanic had rigged the engine to make it run. "Ma'am, you should be good to go until you get the truck turned in tomorrow," he assured her and slammed the hood down.

She wasn't so optimistic. "What's that clinking sound? That can't be normal."

"It's nothing to worry about—only some metal parts rubbing together. It'll stop grinding in a few miles."

"What?" Warning bells sounded in her head. She wasn't a mechanic, by any means, but she knew that this grinding, as he called it, didn't sound good at all.

He pulled a business card from his clipboard and handed it to her. "Ma'am, it won't break down. Trust me. Tell Bobby when you drop off the truck in Magnolia Hill tomorrow to have a look. You shouldn't have any more trouble tonight, but if you do, my number is on the card." He tipped his ball cap at her and walked off.

She texted Maggie to let her know they were on the road again. With her fingers and toes crossed, she put the truck in gear and drove off. "Please, please, please, make it home," she pleaded.

This time, fate was on her side. They pulled up in front of her mom's house just before midnight.

Anna shut off the engine and relaxed into the uncomfortable seat. She couldn't believe it. They were home. She looked over to her sleeping daughter with a smile. "We're here, honey," she whispered, one hand gently shaking her shoulder.

Ashleigh grumbled something and dropped her phone into her book bag.

A female figure in a nightgown walked down the stairs of the well-lit wraparound porch. Anna recognized her right away. She ripped open the driver's side door, jumped down onto the street, and hurried toward Maggie. "Mom!" she said and fell into her arms.

"Oh, Anna," her mom said, her voice cracking. "I'm so glad you two made it home! It's been so long since I've seen you last." Maggie released her from her hug and pointed at the moving truck. "What's that god-awful noise coming from the engine? I thought the road service fixed it?"

"It doesn't matter now. We're here," she said.

Ashleigh dragged her feet on the pavement and yawned. She pulled out one of her earbuds and attempted a smile.

"My oh my, you have grown, Ashleigh," Maggie said and kissed her on the cheek.

Anna laughed when she saw her daughter's shocked face. Ashleigh had never been a hugger, much less a kisser. To her credit, she didn't wipe her face with her T-shirt.

A large bloodhound sauntered toward them to investigate what the commotion was all about and sniffed Ashleigh's hand.

"EEEEEEEEW!" she said in disgust and yanked it away. "He slimed me!"

Maggie laughed. "I see you met Woofus," and as if on cue, the dog howled, as any full-blooded hound would. She handed her a tissue. "You'll get used to the drool."

Ashleigh took it from her and started wiping the goo off her hand. "No, Grandma! That's just gross!"

"Well, let's get you girls situated," she said. "I know it's late, but I made a pot of chili for supper in case you're hungry. If that's too heavy, I also baked a fresh apple pie while I was waiting for you. It's still warm."

"Mom, you're the best," Anna said. "You know I won't be turning down your famous pie."

They dragged their overnight bags upstairs.

Maggie opened the guest room door for them. "Ashleigh, this will be yours," she announced. "It's a tad larger than your mom's, and you'll have a nice view out onto the street."

Anna noticed that the old brown carpet still covered the wooden floor, and that the horrible floral wallpaper had started peeling in the corners. She glanced at Ash, who looked as green as the couch that sat against the wall.

"You're kidding, right?" Ashleigh asked.

Anna laughed. "It'll be all right, sweetie. You can decorate it."

"How about you two give this room a face-lift?" Maggie came to the rescue. "It looks nice, but…"

Ashleigh coughed.

"What I meant to say is that it's outdated, even for my taste. I just didn't have the time or energy to remodel it. So, if you girls don't mind, we could renovate it while school is still out. Ashleigh, you can pick all the colors you want and make the room your own."

Ashleigh grinned. "Thanks, Grandma. Is black and red okay?"

"If that's what you like. Why the heck not?" She turned to Anna. "And you, Anna Maria, you can have your old room back." Maggie opened the door across the hall.

Anna peeked inside and was giddy like a schoolgirl to see her Duran Duran and Wham! posters still hanging on the wall. Even the old quilt Maggie had sewn for her from her favorite dresses covered her bed.

"Mom, you left everything untouched!"

"Darlin', this was your room," Maggie said. "It always will be yours."

Anna opened her closet and jumped up, hoping that what she was looking for was still on that top shelf.

"What are you doing, Mom?" Ashleigh asked.

"You'll see." She had to jump twice. The second time, she glimpsed a corner of it—her treasure chest. "Here, hold this!" Anna handed Ashleigh the comforter that blocked access to the chest, then checked the wall inside the closet. Her old wooden back scratcher still hung on that same hook. She positioned the little hand so it caught the edge of the shoebox that once contained her cross-country cleats. Anna pulled it to the edge of the shelf, then let the box fall into her hands. The lid was dusty.

She opened it, and a wave of nostalgia washed over her. The first thing she saw was her pink faux-leather diary. "You saved it for me!" She ran her fingers over the glitter glue hearts she had painted on the cover as a teenager.

Anna sat the box down on her bed. When she opened the tiny clasp, a small picture fell out and landed on the floor upside down. She picked it up, and her heart began beating twice as fast when she saw who it was of.

"What is it, my dear?" Maggie asked.

Anna held the picture of her once high school sweetheart with both hands to her chest and grinned from ear to ear. With her face warming, she said, "It's Jason."

They were inseparable back then. Even though their relationship didn't survive past their senior prom, he had been such a big part of her life in her teens that just the thought of him gave her warm fuzzies. She closed her eyes. It was good to be home.

* * *

"Let's see what kind of weather we can expect for our region today," the news anchor said. "Chief Meteorologist Jason Morrison, what do you have in store for us today?"

"Well, folks, it will be another hot and

muggy Thursday afternoon in the coastal plains," Jason started. "Nothing unusual for late July, but I have more bad news. It won't get much better if you have plans for the weekend. We'll see a 40 percent chance of afternoon pop-up thunderstorms each day. Some of these storms might become severe. You can expect a high of 98 and a heat index of 104. The low will drop to only 82 overnight. The next cold front that will make its way through Georgia will only cool us down a few degrees. You can expect a short break from the humidity for the next two days. I'd call that good news. Folks, the tropics are calm at the moment, but remember, we're only at the start of the hurricane season. Storms will fire up in the Atlantic in the next few weeks. Don't worry, though, I'll keep a close eye on any tropical developments in the Atlantic and the Gulf Coast for you."

He wrapped up the last loose ends at the station and briefed the evening meteorologist on duty who filled in for him before he got into his truck. Jason usually worked the afternoon and evening broadcasts, but today he had promised Sarah he'd pick her up from the YMCA youth summer program early. The plan was to head straight for a father-daughter date in Savannah, including a trip to the mall to get out of the heat, a dinner, and a movie. He cranked up his AC, rolled the windows down, and drove to the Magnolia Hill Y.

Sarah was already waiting in the shade, alone and reading a book, when he pulled into the parking lot. He opened his driver side door and waved at her. "Sarah!" he called out.

She didn't move.

He honked the horn to get her attention.

Sarah looked up, pulled an earbud out of her ear, and walked toward him. She tossed her backpack in the back seat and climbed up onto the passenger seat. She said nothing, not even a "Hi, Dad."

Jason noticed that she looked more solemn today than on their usual date nights, and he already knew why, because he felt the same pain she did. He worried about her. She had withdrawn from her friends since the accident and isolated herself from others.

"How did your day go?" he asked. Maybe small talk would lighten the mood for both their sakes.

"Why are you wasting your money on making me go to the Y every day? I'm fifteen and don't need a babysitter anymore." She paused, then added, "And the crafts and activities are lame and childish."

Jason sighed. "True. You could stay home, but since it's summer break, I still have to work to make a living. I want you to be around people during at least some of the time I'm working."

"You work evenings."

"My broadcasts are only a small part of my job, and I wish I could spend more time with you," he said. Being a single dad was challenging, especially in his line of work. As the chief meteorologist for the station, he was always on call. On quiet days, he did most of his social media updates, blog entries, and other office-related tasks from home. He also took Sarah with him to community events, but it wasn't enough. Summers were particularly tough because she was out of school, and often afternoon pop-up storms turned severe.

"I understand. It still sucks, though."

"You used to love going to the Y and hanging out with your friends. What happened to them?" he asked. "You girls had sleepovers every weekend."

"They turned dumb and shallow once we started high school. I'd rather be alone than associate with them."

"Okay, so how is Grady? What's he doing this weekend?"

"I don't know. He's busy training for that skateboarding competition in September."

"And? What happened? You two were inseparable growing up. Last time I checked, Grady and his dad still live next door."

"He's got his skater friends, and I like to read books. Those two things don't really go together."

Jason sighed. She used to be a happy-go-lucky, sweet girl. Now she'd lost interest in the things she used to love—all except for reading. "Hey, I have an idea. Why don't we invite Sean and Grady over to throw some burgers on the grill tomorrow evening?"

"Whatever you say," she said.

He shot her a stern look. She never talked to him like that. Her indifference was so out of character for his daughter, and he began to worry. "Tell me about it?" he asked.

She shook her head, then reconsidered. "I miss her, Dad," she said, close to tears.

"I miss her, too, sweetheart." Today marked two years since a drunk driver hit their car and killed his wife, Caroline. He squeezed Sarah's hand and tried to comfort her the only way he could. "You know, I think your mom would want us to be happy instead of moping around with sad faces all the time, don't you think?"

Sarah lowered her head. "I know. It's just so hard not having her with us. I sometimes feel as if she's with me. I dream of her every night."

"So do I," Jason said. "Your mom was a special person, and I'll never forget her." He paused for a moment and lifted Sarah's chin up with his hand. "Listen to me, Sarah. You mean the world to me. It's okay to be sad, and as hard as it is, we have to find things to live for instead of just barely making it through the day. Mom would want us to make new memories and enjoy life again, don't you think?"

"You go first," she said. A fraction of a smile pulled on one corner of her mouth.

He laughed. "Oh, no! Don't you ever use my wise words against me!"

She was adorable when she tried to hide her natural sunshine and failed. That realization reminded him that he would do anything to see his daughter happy again.

"We need some music." Sarah took the other earbud out of her ear and turned on the car stereo. She rolled her eyes at the classic rock station he'd had on before and changed it to a country station. "Much better!"

"Really?" This time, he rolled his eyes. Country made him cringe, but today was a special day.

"I remember Mom and I two-stepping through the house when we did chores or waited for a cake to bake in the oven."

"So do I." If listening to country music made Sarah feel better, so be it. He loved his daughter with all of his heart, and she'd been through enough. He could live with sadness until his time was up, but Sarah still had her entire life ahead of her. She deserved to be happy. "So, let's go shopping at the mall." He tapped his thumbs on the steering wheel and started singing along with the song. He knew he sounded like a bloodhound howling on a wraparound porch.

Sarah laughed and pretended to cover her ears. "Dad, no...don't!"

Chapter 2

"Girls, I'm heading over to the shop for a few hours. I need to order more baby yarn and knitting supplies. We are in the middle of a mini baby boom." Maggie smiled. "Lots of young couples in Magnolia Hill like to snuggle up during the winter months, and you know what happens next." She winked at Anna. "I love it, because come spring and summer, every woman in town is either related to or knows someone who's having a baby. It's good for business. If ya'll want to come with me for a spell and have a look-see, I'd love to show you around."

"I will," Anna said, and shot a glare at Ashleigh.

"Okay, I'm coming, too," she mumbled.

"That's wonderful." Maggie's smile dropped to a frown as if she was embarrassed. "I have to admit that baby season is Spinning Yarns' main source of income, which I also admit is not quite as lucrative as it sounds. I can barely keep the shop doors open. I think crafts are not as popular as they used to be. People are busy with work, and nowadays it's easier to buy gifts online than make them yourself. Maybe you can help me come up with some ideas to drum up business. The shop has seen better days, and I'm afraid it needs some work."

"Like my room?" Ashleigh asked.

Maggie nodded. "Yes, baby girl, like your room."

Anna's heart ached for her mom. The old Spinning Yarns craft shop was buzzing with activity when she grew up. Women of all ages used to gather in the shop in the evenings to work on their projects and to gossip about the latest town scandals. It must be bad when even her always-optimistic mother had doubts. "No worries, Mom. We'll have a look and figure out how to make Spinning Yarns a community hang-out for our ladies, and maybe even some interested men, again. I'm ready to go see it when you are."

"I'm ready, too. Come on, Woofus," Maggie said, patting the side of her leg. "Let's take a walk."

Woofus grunted and laid his head

between his front paws on the kitchen floor. He wasn't going anywhere.

Anna couldn't blame him. "You don't wanna go out in this heat, do you?"

His droopy eyes pleaded.

"Me neither." She scraped the last crumbs off her plate and put her dishes in the sink. "But Ashleigh and I need to get acclimated. So, walking it is."

The hound exhaled through his jowls, which flapped on the linoleum floor, then he slowly stretched, got up, and walked to the door.

The store was only two blocks from Maggie's house. Anna was far from used to the heat and the humidity that awaited them outside during what seemed to be the hottest and muggiest day in Georgia history. How she managed running around the woods all day in the middle of summer as a child was a mystery to her. She'd be ready to head back inside in less than five minutes if she tried it now.

Ten minutes later, they stood in front of the Spinning Yarns shop. Sweat ran down Anna's back and made her T-shirt stick to her skin. "Gross," she said as she tugged on her shirt to unglue it from her back. A glass of iced tea and air conditioning sounded like heaven right about now.

Thunder rumbled in the distance as Maggie unlocked the front door. Anna looked up. The thin wisps of white streaking the blue summer sky were already puffing up to form larger, towering popcorn clouds.

Turning her attention back to the storefront, she realized her mom was right about the condition of the shop.

The window frames and signs looked faded, chipped, and in desperate need of a fresh new look. "Ashleigh, you're good with paint. You could do the lettering for the display window, while I do the big, easy stuff that doesn't need pretty handwriting," she said.

Ashleigh shrugged, but Anna could tell she had piqued her interest.

"I know, it doesn't look as inviting as it used to..." Maggie said, her fair cheeks flushing. "I've just had no energy lately. It must be this heat."

Anna worried about her mother's health. She didn't want her to end up like some of her patients whose quality of life had deteriorated because they ignored early warning signs. Maggie had always been active. Most days, she had enough energy for both of them. If she wasn't working at the shop, she was at home cooking and baking up a storm. Today, Anna could tell she wasn't feeling well. Something wasn't right. "Have you told Doc Porter about this?"

Maggie waved her off. "No worries. He said it's just a touch of sugar and to take it easy on the sweets."

"Mom!" She rested her hand on Maggie's arm. "You've got to take this seriously! This is not something you can ignore and hope it gets better."

Maggie gave her a no-nonsense glare. "Doc Porter knows what he's talking about. I don't need you to lecture me."

Taken aback, Anna let go of her arm and raised both hands. "All right, Mom. I'll let you off the hook today, but we'll need to talk about this. Promise?" She held her mother's glare and waited.

Maggie sighed. "One day."

"One day, as in tonight?"

"One day."

"Good." Happy with at least the possibility of a talk about her health, she entered the store and looked around. "It's not that bad, Mom. The shop looks dark, but I think simple things like better lighting, a lighter shade of paint on the walls, and new decorations can make a big difference." Her eyes caught on an old poster of a model wearing an '80s sweater. "These ancient advertisements have to go!"

"I like the way you think. Truth is, those posters have been hanging on the walls so long that I didn't even notice them anymore." Maggie walked over to a large table. "What about our craft nook? I think it needs something."

"It looks like a third-grade art table," the teenager chimed in.

"Ashleigh!"

"No, I'm serious, Mom." She walked over to the plastic tables with the folding chairs tucked under. "Think of a bookstore. They create hangouts for their customers so they spend more time in the store. This increases the chance that they buy something even though they didn't think they needed it. You could use the same strategy with Spinning Yarns."

"We could do some yard sale hunting for some comfortable armchairs to put in the corners," Anna suggested. "What about looking for a large wooden table and chairs at an estate sale? We can keep the folding furniture for overflow and outdoor events. The chairs don't have to match, but it would make this space more inviting.”

“You also should set up a side table with fresh coffee and a few small treats. Add a few decorative lamps in the corners, you know, so people have a reason to bring their crafts and hang out.”

“...the way Spinning Yarns used to be, when I was growing up,” Anna added to her daughter’s comments. “We can help you get this place in tip-top shape. Ashleigh is out of school for another week and I’m still job hunting.” Anna would love to run the store with her mom full-time. It’d always been her dream when she was young, but right now, the shop’s revenue couldn’t support all three of them.

“Grandma?” Ashleigh waved an event calendar printout in the air. “Do teenagers live in this town or only old people?"

"Ashleigh!" Anna couldn't believe her daughter had that much cheek, then grabbed a copy to see for herself. "Uh, Mom, I think she has a point."

"What do you mean?"

"If you want this shop to survive, you need to add some cool crafts and patterns. Nobody wants to knit potholders or outdated sweaters. Who even wears sweaters down here? Does it even get cold enough in the winter?"

"Oh, so what do you suggest?"

"Well, let's use local teenagers as an example," Ashleigh said. "We want stuff that reminds us of books and movies. Fan things. Things that mean something to us, not potholders. I can draw something up for you. I'll be bored to tears anyway until school starts."

Anna's heart skipped a beat. "Way to go, Ashleigh, for taking initiative," she said, careful not to act too excited. Ashleigh had always been artistic, so this would be right up her alley. "So, that covers your teens," Anna added. "Now we just need to get the moms of Magnolia Hill excited. We should develop some cool ideas for them. Do you have a website, Mom?"

Maggie shook her head. "I don't know how to do all that technical stuff."

"We got you covered, Grandma!"

Maggie couldn't contain her joy. She grabbed Ashleigh's face with both hands and kissed her on each cheek. "You girls are a blessing!"

Anna laughed as she watched her daughter recoil.

A delivery truck parked in front of the store and a burly man in his forties rolled up a hand truck with boxes stacked on top of each other.

Anna opened the door for him. "Hello!" she said. "Are these for us?"

"Hi, and yes," the delivery man said, pulling the load onto the sidewalk.

"Thank you, ma'am," he said as he wheeled the boxes into the shop and into a corner out of customers' way. "Is this a good place, or do you want them somewhere else?"

"This is fine," she said.

"Where's Mr. Brown today?" Maggie asked.

"He's a little under the weather," he said as he turned the empty hand truck around. "Mr. Brown might be out for a few weeks, so Magnolia Hill will have to put up with me for a while." He chuckled as he walked toward the door. "Those are some very large shoes to fill, and the owner of Mamaw's already made certain I understood where everything goes. Lucky for me, the pretty waitress had pity on me and helped me out."

"You mean Beth?" Maggie asked.

"Yes, at least that's the name on her tag. We didn't get to talk much because of the laser beams the boss lady aimed at us."

"That's Roberta for you." Maggie shook her head and opened a box. "She's what you call a bit old-fashioned, somewhat dragon-like, if you get my drift. Beth, on the other hand, is sweet and could never hurt a soul. She needs a man who is kind to her after that no-good husband of hers..."

Anna cleared her throat to rescue the poor delivery man from her mother's matchmaking. "My name is Anna, by the way." She reached her hand out to him.

He released one hand from the hand truck and shook hers. The firm grip almost crushed her tender bones. "Kevin."

It took quite an effort not to show her pain from her hand. Instead, she grinned and pointed at Maggie. "This is my mother, Maggie Weaver," she replied through gritted teeth and sighed with relief when he released her aching hand. "She owns the shop."

Maggie waved. "That's me," she said, turning her attention back to unpacking the boxes.

Kevin nodded. "Yes, ma'am. You have a wonderful shop."

Anna felt an awkward silence hang in the air.

Kevin nodded. "Well, ladies, it's very nice to meet you, but I have lots more deliveries," he said and headed toward the door.

"Tell Roberta and Beth I said hello when you see them on your next delivery," Maggie said.

"I certainly will, ma'am," he said, about to leave.

"One more thing before you go," Maggie said, looking Kevin in the eyes, putting on that sweet-as-honey smile of hers.

Anna knew what was coming.

"Beth is a sweet woman with a heart of gold. She had a tough life, Kevin, and deserves someone who's good to her. Just keep that in mind."

"Yes, ma'am!" he said. "Understood." He nodded at them both one more time and left.

Anna shook her head as the truck drove off. "You're impossible, Mom."

Maggie grinned in return. "What? Planting a little bug won't hurt." She took a deep breath and turned somber. "Listen, Anna. I appreciate any way you can help with the shop. I would hate to close this place down and retire. Running this shop is my life. It gives me purpose. I just don't think the younger crowd likes to knit or crochet anymore."

Anna smiled. "I do, and Ashleigh loved knitting scarves and hats for the Colorado winters and cute accessories for the summer."

"I wish other teens were as artsy as Ash," Maggie sighed. "If this trend keeps up, knitting will be a lost skill."

"Not if we can help it, Mom," Anna said. "I have some ideas…"

* * *

A loud siren blared in the back of the shop.

Anna clutched her heart and then realized it was the weather radio. She never owned one in Colorado but knew that she'd have to get used to the sound again, living in a severe weather-prone area.

"A tornado watch has been issued for the following counties until five p.m.," the voice crackled over the speaker.

"Here we go, Anna! Did you miss the stormy weather?"

Anna grinned. "Actually, I did." She remembered going storm chasing with Jason and their friends Sean, Miles, and Jenna when they were in high school. Other than playing Dungeons & Dragons on weekends, chasing tornadoes and driving into hurricanes to experience the power of nature was their favorite pastime back then. The adrenaline rush from chasing deadly storms was a thrill like no other, especially when they all thought they were invincible. Even a few close calls couldn't make them act less daring. *Stupid teenagers*, she thought—and she had been one of them. Of course, their parents never knew about their little deadly adventures.

Jason had always been the weather-smart one of the group. He read all the meteorological-related books he could get his hands on in the library. Then he also had this knack of knowing where storms would go and if they were worth chasing by looking at the clouds and taking in every clue

Mother Nature gave him. Everyone else was just along for the ride. Before every chase, Sean would drive them to a large field where Jason did his weather psychic voodoo thing, then they'd figure out a plan of action. One day, as he studied the storm clouds, he wrapped his arm around her shoulders and pointed at angry looking cloud structures, explaining what he thought was going to happen with a particular storm cell. That moment, lightning wasn't the only spark that flew. It was the moment when everything changed. No longer were they only friends—they were in love.

Back then, Anna was convinced that they'd spend the rest of their lives together. Not only was he smart, loved storms, and made her world spin with his kisses, he also knew her better than anyone else in the world. After all, their first playdate was building castles in a sandbox together. Life, however, had other plans for them, and she came to accept the fact, even though it hurt.

Jason was probably married now. Good for him. Every so often, when times were tough in her own marriage, she had thought of their time together. She'd wonder how things would have turned out if Jason hadn't broken up with her before heading off to college. As a then-married woman, she always pushed that thought away as fast as it came. She couldn't change things that were never meant to be, anyway.

A flash of lightning illuminated the shop, followed by a loud clap of thunder that made the electrical outlets pop. Anna jumped out of her skin and held her hand to her chest. "That was close!"

Maggie turned on the small TV in the back of the shop. "Folks, we have an important weather update for you. We have a few strong cells that popped up over our region that could spin out a tornado at any time," the voice on TV said. It sounded pretty darn familiar.

No way! she thought. Just to make sure she heard right, she took a step closer to the TV and stared at the screen. "Jason? He's moved back?"

"That he did," Maggie said. "He's been working at the station for about ten years. He's the chief weatherman," she added.

"Meteorologist, Mom." She stared at the TV screen. A wave of nostalgia coursed from her head to her toes. He hadn't changed a bit, just looked grown up now. Jason kept his dark-blond hair short and stylish, and his smile still drew her in.

"You could meet up with him to catch up," Maggie suggested.

"Yeah, I could," she said, trying not to let on that she was spellbound. Then she saw his wedding band and her nostalgic bubble burst with one giant pop. "Of course, he's married." She walked away from the TV to the front of the shop to watch the mayhem that was unfolding outside.

The wind rattled the old glass door and windows, and debris was flying down Main Street. Anna watched the decorative crepe myrtle trees stretch and bend to the mercy of the storm. It was just a matter of time before one of them snapped in half. She could feel her pulse race. "This is intense!" Anna felt the adrenaline surge through her body.

The weather radio's alarm sounded again. "A severe thunderstorm warning has been issued…"

 "All right, Anna," Maggie said. "I know you want to watch the storm, but I'd feel much better if you'd join us in the back where it's safer and wait this storm out. The last thing we need is you getting cut all over if the glass breaks."

Anna tore her gaze from the flying debris and joined her family. Maggie was right. As much as she wanted to keep watching, she now had responsibilities, mainly Ashleigh. She also couldn't afford the medical bill if she got hurt.

"Folks," Jason's voice sounded from the TV.

All three stopped to listen to Jason's update.

Despite the ring, Anna couldn't take her eyes off him. She would never entertain getting between a man and his marriage, but it was nice to dream a little.

"If you have a weather radio, you already know we now have a severe thunderstorm warning issued for Liberty County. Magnolia Hill residents, watch out! You'll have a humdinger on your doorstep for the next ten to fifteen minutes. This cell is intensifying as we speak and is slowly moving east. Expect lots of rain, some quarter-size hail, and remember, we're still under a tornado watch until five o'clock tonight. I recommend you stay close to your weather radio or download our weather app so you can get instant weather warnings and take shelter in your safe space."

"Too bad you're already taken," she whispered, barely audible.

"What's that?" Maggie asked.

"Oh, nothing." This was just her luck. Not that she was looking for someone to date, anyway. Her ex-husband almost strangled her to death before the divorce. She didn't need a man in her life again who'd keep reminding her she wasn't good enough, that she wasn't worthy. Not that Jason had ever made her feel that way when they were high school sweethearts, or even before then when they were just friends in grade school. He never disrespected her. Nevertheless, she had more important things to worry about, such as getting herself and Ashleigh settled. Dreaming about someone who once was the love of her life and was now taken would only distract her.

Chapter 3

After sitting down for dinner the next day, Anna could barely move. "Good night. I'm going to bed," she called out, as she dragged her exhausted body up the stairs to her room.

Traveling across the country and getting settled took everything she had out of her. Every muscle in her body was sore from emptying the U-Haul and dragging all their stuff upstairs and into storage a storage unit she had rented. She plopped on her bed, then looked around her old room. A few leftover boxes stood piled high on top of each other in a corner. She frowned. They blocked most of her posters and memorabilia. One item from her youth, however, she'd kept close last night.

Anna pressed her lips together in pain as she reached over to her old diary on the nightstand. "I swear, I'm never moving again...well, after I move out of here," she mumbled and yawned. Her eyes burned, and she could barely keep them open. She flipped through the tattered journal and began to read an entry somewhere close to the middle.

A few pages in, she had to giggle at her feeble attempts to use code to describe how in love she was with Jason. She hadn't wanted her mom to find the diary by accident one day and read all about her private thoughts and dreams she had for Jason or what they were doing when they were together. For example, sharing ice cream in her diary was code for kissing. They shared a lot of ice cream in only the first few entries she had read so far.

A couple of entries later, Anna caught herself nodding off, while reading an entry that recounted a night out with Jason at the Magnolia Hill drive-in theater. Too stubborn to close the diary for the night, she re-read the same paragraph for the third time. She and Jason had been so wrapped up in "eating ice cream" that they'd missed what was happening on the silver screen. A knock on the car window had interrupted their passionate ice cream eating.

Suddenly, Anna's eyes flew open with a start as she found her face planted on the open pages of her diary. She knew when she was beat. "Okay, I give up," she conceded as she closed the diary and set it back on the nightstand. She turned off the light, molded her pillow to cradle her head, and shut her eyes.

As she drifted off to sleep, the last entry of her diary replayed in her mind, uncensored this time. Once more, they were so engaged in their kiss that they had forgotten the world around them. Then, there was the knock on the window again, but something was wrong.

It was Luke, her now ex-husband.

How did he get there? *This surely must be a bad dream,* she thought. She wanted to push him out of her dream, but she couldn't. All she could do was let the scene unfold.

His evil grin chilled her to the bone.

"Hey! What are you doing with my wife?"

Her surroundings shifted, and now it was only Luke and her in their old Colorado home with her backed against a wall. He raised his hands to her neck. "You ruined everything!" His breath reeked of chewing tobacco. She wanted to run, but she was paralyzed with fear.

When his hands squeezed her neck, she finally woke with an achy throat and clammy hands. Her breath was fast and erratic. Her room was pitch black except for the moon shining through the tree branches in front of her window. She rubbed her throat with her hand. "It was just a dream... just a dream," she told herself to try to calm down. "I'm okay." Yet, it had felt so real.

Still reeling from her nightmare, she turned on her light, flipped to the page in her diary where she had dozed off, and finished reading the entry. This time, there was indeed a knock on the car window. Anna held her breath. But instead of Luke, it was her best friend, Jenna, with her boyfriend in tow, wanting to know if they would meet them at the diner after the movie.

Anna closed the diary again. Relieved, she let her head plop back onto her overstuffed pillow. It's over, she told herself. So why did Luke still have so much power over her? The divorce was final, and she had a restraining order against him. Too bad it didn't extend to dreams. She turned off the light in hopes of getting a few more hours of peaceful sleep.

* * *

The next morning, Anna woke to the smell something delicious cooking downstairs. Memories of childhood Sunday mornings flooded her senses. She checked her alarm clock. Her mom must have been at the early church service and was back already. Beckoned by the wonderful aroma, she got out of bed and walked down the stairs.

"Hey, Mom," Ashleigh said, already dressed and attacking a stack of pancakes with butter and syrup. "Grandma is taking me to the mall in Savannah."

"I figured you could use some alone time, Anna." Maggie sat a plate with a sunny-side up egg and bacon in front of her. "Pancake? Biscuit and gravy?"

"Thanks, Mom, but I don't have a big enough stomach to eat all that!"

"Of course, you can, sweetie," she said, stacking two pancakes on a separate plate for her and poured a steady stream of syrup on top.

"Mom!"

Ashleigh laughed. "I wouldn't mind eating breakfast like this every day."

"Yeah, you have the metabolism of a flea. I, as you can see, am allergic to carbs. They make me break out in fat all over."

Maggie laughed. "I'll remember to make less next time. Today, let me spoil you two a little."

"Don't mind my mom, Grandma. It's perfectly fine with me."

"Okay, already. I'll have a plate." Anna tasted the delicious and soft sweetness of her pancakes. Her mom always added a hint of cinnamon to the batter, which gave her recipe a unique touch. She often wished she had inherited Maggie's gift for cooking and baking. Her lack of skill was even more frustrating when she tried to cook for other people. She had resigned herself to the fact that her talent lay in eating the wonderful food others made and then showering the chefs and bakers with compliments.

Anna glanced over at Ashleigh and watched her finish her last bite of pancake, scraping up the buttery syrup with her fork. It was good to see her daughter laugh again. Even though Anna was home, she hoped Ashleigh would one day forgive her for ripping her from hers and moving them to Magnolia Hill.

Half an hour later, Anna was alone. She sat at the kitchen table, contemplating what to do next. The afternoon was hers. Some TLC would be a good start. Anna went upstairs, almost tripping over Woofus, gathered up some Georgia-appropriate clothes to wear, and headed for the bathroom. She set out her razor, shaving cream, tweezers, nail polish remover, and her favorite fuchsia shade of polish. When she glanced at the mirror, Anna looked away as feelings of shame and guilt washed over her. How could she let herself go like this? Maybe Luke was right. She was fat now, and nobody would want someone like her.

No, she did not want to start her new life feeling bad for herself. She may not be slender at the moment, but at least she could work with what she had—a pretty face, lush brown waves, and a cute smile. Although she was overweight, she also had nice curves in all the right places. Most important, she was still alive, for which she was forever grateful.

After she shaved and showered, and cleaned up her brows, she removed her chipped polish from her toenails and put on a couple of fresh coats of the fuchsia polish. The bright color instantly lifted her mood. If she could ever afford it, she vowed to splurge on getting regular pedicures at a salon, especially in the summer months. For now, she'd have to do it herself.

Even though it was already in the upper eighties outside, she still felt cool and refreshed from her lukewarm shower. She blow-dried her hair, put on a little makeup, and did a last-minute check in the mirror. Her reflection smiled back at her. Not too bad. With renewed confidence, she returned to her bedroom and tackled a few more boxes.

Halfway through the second box, the doorbell rang and Woofus barked.

"Hello? Anybody home? Anna!" a female voice called out.

Anna walked down the steps toward the front door. That voice sounded familiar. "I'm coming!" she called out. She almost ran when she saw her best friend standing outside the screen door with a pastry box in one hand. As soon as her friend saw her, she ripped the screen door open, and they fell into each other's arms.

"Jenna! Gosh, it's been so long!" Anna squeezed her a little tighter. "I missed you so much!" With both of them leading busy lives, they had lost touch over the years.

"It's been too long." Jenna handed her the pink and blue box with a big red cherry on it. "Maggie came by the shop last week and mentioned you were on your way to Magnolia Hill, so of course I had to come see you. I brought you cupcake samples from my bakery. These are some of my best-selling ones. I hope you'll like them."

Anna took the box from her. "Cherry on Top Cupcake Shop—I love the name," she said. Her mouth began to water just thinking of the goodness inside. Anna peeked through the clear lid, and the contents didn't disappoint. "Wow, Jenna, they look wonderful. You've always had a knack for baking. Me, on the other hand..."

"Oh, stop it! I'm here to abduct you. How about I take you out for some heavenly pie at Mamaw's Diner?" Jenna took her by the arm and dragged her out the front door. "I know it's a little late for lunch, but you should try Roberta's Sunday roast one day. It's to die for. Anyway, we have so much to talk about."

Anna looked down at her clothes. "Wait, let me change into a blouse and some nicer sandals, and I'll be all yours. I don't want to stick out like a sore thumb when everybody is dressed in their Sunday best," she called on her way back up the porch stairs. "That's all I need—the whole town talking about how sloppy I've become..."

Her friend laughed. "Come on, you know they'll talk, regardless of what you wear."

"You have a point. Why bother," Anna said. "I do need to grab my purse, though."

Jenna let go of her arm. "Hurry! I want to catch up and gossip, now that you're finally home again. Let this be the first of many more pie dates to come."

"You better believe it."

Chapter 4

When they arrived at the diner, there were more people leaving Mamaw's than entering. It was a good sign that the masses of church goers were off to other events or naps, leaving them with a quiet place to talk.

"Good timing," Jenna said.

From the corner of her eye, Anna caught the lit-up glass case that held a variety of glistening pies and colorful cupcakes. Her eyes bounced between her favorite, the apple pie, and a cupcake with pink and purple icing topped with matching sprinkles. Like a powerful magnet, Anna followed the pull to the dessert case. "Oh, I think I know what I want," she said, trying to reign in her enthusiasm with little success.

"The cupcakes are from my shop," Jenna said with a slight blush.

It took Anna extra willpower to tear her gaze from the wonderful, sweet desserts. She wiped her thumb over the corner of her mouth down to her chin, just to make sure she wasn't drooling before she turned to face her friend. "Wow, you must make a killing selling them here. There's only a couple cupcakes left on display."

Jenna's face flushed. "Well, they are popular. Let's just say, I'm not starving," she said, followed with a reserved giggle. "Mind you, I work long hours to run my baking business, but the ice cream shop and a few other stores in town are also selling them, which helps."

"I'm so happy things are working out for you here. Now you only need a Prince Charming who treats you like a princess."

"I've been tryin' to tell her for years," a cheerful female voice said in a heavy southern accent behind her.

Anna turned around to find a slender woman about her age wearing her hair in a cute updo and holding a pen and pad. "I'll be darned! If that isn't Anna Weaver!" the woman said and threw herself at her.

She looked familiar, but Anna couldn't figure out who she was.

"It sure is," Jenna said. "Anna, I'm sure you remember Beth Milligan from school. She graduated two years after us. She's Miles Milligan's sister."

That's right; she'd almost forgot that Maggie mentioned her at the shop when Kevin delivered the boxes of yarn. When Beth released her, Anna stepped back to take a second look. "Wow, Beth, you're all grown up!" Her facial features had also matured and filled out some— maybe that's why she didn't recognize her at first. She remembered her as the annoying, geeky kid. Beth always wanted to hang out with her and her friends when they played Dungeons & Dragons and watched movies on VHS together.

"And she's mellowed out a lot," Jenna added.

"Stop it, Jenna! I wasn't that bad."

Both, Anna and Jenna nodded in unison.

"Oh, yes, you were," Jenna said and drew her into an apologetic hug. "But I do love you, quirks and all!"

"I'm not sure how to take that," Beth said, "so I'll assume it was a compliment."

Telling Beth about her secret delivery guy admirer, Kevin, was tempting, but Anna decided it was best to stay out of their business. Unlike Maggie, she had never been a successful matchmaker and didn't want to ruin Beth's potential love life.

"Let's find you a table. Mamaw is already giving me that evil look."

Anna glanced toward the counter, and sure enough, the old woman was throwing daggers with her eyes at them.

Beth seated them at a booth by the

window. "What can I bring ya'll to drink?" she asked.

"Sweet tea," they replied in unison and giggled.

"This feels just like old times, doesn't it?" Jenna clapped her hands in joy.

"Have ya'll decided what you want to order, or should I check back in a few minutes?" Beth asked.

Anna's mind traveled back twenty-plus years in the past as she listened to Beth's southern accent. *Yes, this is home*, she thought, *where Sunday lunch is dinner, and dinner is supper.* "Ma'am, I hear the banana puddn' is to die for," she said with exaggerated politeness. "I'll take that with some of your apple pie and vanilla ice cream." Anna then glared at Jenna and said, "Don't judge!" and gave her a sweet-as-sugar smile. Returning her attention back to Beth, she said, "And if you could box up that pink and purple cupcake to go... I want to take it home to my mom."

As soon as the lie left Anna's lips, blood rushed to her head. If they only knew that her morning had already started with a huge syrupy pancake...

"Only if you don't judge me," Jenna countered, then also turned her attention to Beth. "And I'll have the red velvet cake and a birthday cake malt." Jenna leaned over and whispered loud enough for Beth to hear, "We both know that cupcake is for you."

Beth winked at Anna. "I'll be right back with your desserts," she said and weaved around the tables toward the display case.

"I'm so glad you moved back home," Jenna said.

"Me, too! I needed to be with family after what happened. It was time." There it was: the elephant in the room. Both went silent. Anna had poured her heart out more than once on the phone with Jenna since the incident. Today was not about her hardship. It was about celebrating their reunion and catching up. "Enough about me. What happened to Mikey after I left?"

"We married and divorced," Jenna said. "He was a dork and more interested in football and beer than me. Thank God I didn't have kids with him." Jenna took a sip of her tea and continued. "My soul mate is out there somewhere. Hopefully I'll find him before I'm too old to have kids."

Anna sensed a bit of sadness in her friend's voice. "I'm sure there is, and Mr. Right is probably thinking the same thing about his luck in love."

Jenna took another sip of tea. "First, we gotta catch you up on all the juicy gossip."

Anna leaned forward, all ears. "Do tell!"

"Let's see. Where to start... Oh yeah, do you remember Leslie Morgan, the cheerleader? She is pregnant with her sixth child." Jenna shrugged her shoulders. "Her and Tony Jackson got married about eight years ago and have been making babies ever since. Can you imagine? When I see the two and their brood, I keep thanking the Lord that I'm single and have no kids, at least for the time being."

"So much for her cheerleading career," Anna mused. "My guess is she never went to the University of Georgia."

"Nope."

"Let's see, what else..." Jenna continued. "So are you going to get in touch with Jason now that you're a free woman?" Jenna asked with a supposed innocent grin pasted on her face. "He's the weather guy for one of the local channels and famous around these parts of Georgia."

Anna blushed. "I know, I saw him on TV when we had the tornado watch yesterday. But no, I don't think it would be a good idea."

Jenna frowned. "Why not? I'm sure he would love seeing you again."

"Not a chance! He's married, and I don't need to torture myself by reliving old memories." She'd already done enough strolling down memory lane.

Jenna's cheerful facial expression fell.

"What?"

"You don't know? He lost his wife after some drunk teenager hit her car head-on after she picked up their daughter from a friend's house," she said with a somber tone of voice.

"Oh?" Anna hadn't expected to hear that.

"She died two years ago. Both were grieving for a long time."

Anna's chest tightened with her own grief. She'd never lost a close family member, but she'd missed having a dad. From the stories Maggie had told her, Rafael and her mother were inseparable. When Maggie became pregnant, Rafael had promised to marry her. "I can work double-shifts at the diner to support our baby," he had said. Then one day, he up and left town only a few weeks before Anna was born. She never knew what it was like to have a dad.

"So how are you doing?" Jenna asked.

"Aw, Jenna," she began. "The divorce was difficult, but I did have wonderful support from my work friends. My ambulance partner, Dan, and his wife took me and Ash in after the house sold and all the legal stuff was wrapped up. They also collected up some money at the fire station for us as a going-away gift."

"That's wonderful."

"I'm still having nightmares from when he strangled me, but I'm healing. Once I'm working again, I'll continue with my counseling."

"Anna, know I'm here for you, no matter what." Jenna's eyes glistened, then she blinked. "How's your daughter adjusting to the move? Is she still upset about leaving Colorado?"

Anna hung her head and sighed. "I'm worried about her, Jenna. She didn't want to leave her friends, and it will be difficult for her to adjust to living in the country."

"I get that."

"She still wants to move back and live with Luke, even after what happened. The court granted me sole custody of Ash, but I won't risk him putting her in danger. She blames me for everything. In a twisted kind of way, I think I could have prevented this entire ordeal somehow."

"Listen to yourself, Anna Weaver! He's a controlling and dangerous man. Luke kept you two away from your family for all these years, then he strangled you because he was mad that you caught him cheating in your own home. He made the decision to betray you, and he lashed out at you. It wasn't your fault."

"I know. I just wish Ashleigh didn't have to suffer like this and that she'll realize that small-town living can have its advantages. She hates me." Anna felt as if someone had squeezed her heart like a lemon. Would her daughter ever forgive her?

Jenna reached out to her hand and held it in hers. "It'll be okay. Trust me. And if you need to talk, I'll be right here for you, okay?"

Anna nodded. "Thanks, Jenna. You've always been my best friend."

"Family Fun & Movies at the Park" had become a mid-August summer favorite for the people of Magnolia Hill in the last ten years. Food trucks, bounce houses for the little ones, and a local band entertained the crowd until it was dark enough for the movie to start.

"Sarah, grab the blankets for us. And Grady, will you carry that beach bag?" Jason asked and picked up the folding chairs.

Jason had always looked forward to spending time with Sarah and Caroline at the summer event. It just wasn't the same without his wife, but they kept the tradition going anyway. He enjoyed catching up with friends he hadn't seen in a few months with a beer or two until it was time to settle down and watch the movie.

As they walked toward the stage, the Boonie-Boys, a local bluegrass band, already entertained the crowds with a washboard, spoons, and bass. The dance floor was crowded with young and old alike having a good time moving to the upbeat music.

"How about this spot?" Grady pointed at an area where a few others had already set up their chairs for the movie.

"Excellent! Let's make sure we have enough room for your dad when he gets here."

"I just texted him. He said he'll meet us in about an hour."

Jason sat the folding chairs on the grass and started pulling them out of their covers. "Just in time for the movie to start," he replied. "I'm glad he's able to make it tonight." Grady's dad, Sean, had been busy ever since becoming sheriff. Jason tried to include Grady in family events more often, even though Sarah and Grady had grown apart from being childhood friends. Still, two single dads had to help each other out in all matters parenting. Most of the time, these sessions involved a barbecue grill and a few beers on the weekend.

"So, Grady, how was your first week back in school? Did you get the classes and teachers you wanted?" Jason asked.

"Yeah, for the most part. Sarah and I are taking English and social science together. History is going to suck, though. Mr. Spinner already gave us a pop quiz. Who does that in the first week?"

"Did you pass?" Jason asked.

"Nope. First week back from summer break is supposed to be easy."

Sarah rolled her eyes at her friend. "Grady, I warned you about Mr. Spinner. I told you when we got our schedules he's no joke."

Jason swatted at a mosquito that tried to land on his arm. It was a typical summer evening, still hot and muggy. The mosquitos would try to eat him alive as soon as the sun disappeared behind the trees. Jason had taken his own advice from the midday forecast and packed plenty of bug spray for the event. He dug out the repellant and applied a liberal amount of the spray, making himself and everyone within a few feet of him cough. "Kids, be sure to put on some bug spray. The skeeters are already out."

"I think we're good, Dad," Sarah said, still struggling to breathe. "You already made sure the entire park is wearing some. Can we get dinner now? I'm getting hungry."

"Let's finish setting up, then we can look around and hit the food trucks," he said. Supporting the local vendors at events like this was important to him, and, as a public figure, it was almost expected of him to be a good example. He didn't mind.

"Kids, spread out the chairs just a little more," Jason instructed. When he was happy with the arrangement, he moved the beach bag between the chairs. "Come on, you two. Let's go get some grub."

They walked over to one of the food trucks. "Three hot dogs, two nachos, one water, and two cokes," Jason said when it was his turn to order their dinner. He handed Sarah the drinks and Grady grabbed the nachos. Jason paid the volunteer, picked up the hot dogs, and backed away from the line.

"Dad! Watch out!" Sarah called out.

Jason turned, and he could feel cold liquid run down his back, followed by a gasp and a splash behind him. He looked around and realized that he had backed into a woman who also had her hands full of food.

"Oh, wow," said a teenage girl in a black T-shirt with a skateboard printed on it standing next to the woman. She looked about Sarah's age.

He looked down and found a muddy mess of upside-down nachos in a sea of cheese and soda. "I'm so sorry! I'll buy you a new meal." He looked at her shirt and noticed a trail of nacho cheese ran down the length of it. He could feel the heat rising to his face. "I'll get your shirt cleaned, too."

He piled the hot dogs on Sarah and Grady's stacks of food and drinks, then grabbed extra napkins. He wanted to wipe the mess off her shirt, but then realized that it was highly inappropriate. Instead, he handed her the napkins and dug out his wallet. He pulled out two twenties. "Will forty dollars be enough for dry cleaning? I'm really sorry this happened."

"It's okay," she said. "It's an old shirt, and I can just wipe it with a napkin."

"Oh, no, I insist." He handed her the money, and for the first time made eye contact. Wait, she looked familiar. No, it couldn't be! "Anna?"

Her face brightened. "Jason!"

It was her. He couldn't believe his eyes. She was still as beautiful as he remembered. "Are you visiting your mom?"

"No, I just moved back to town a few weeks ago."

"Oh, yeah?" He was thrilled to hear the good news. Every so often, he would wonder how Anna was doing. Maggie sometimes watched Sarah when he had to work odd hours during severe weather events. She had told him that Anna was married, had a daughter, and that she was a paramedic. That surprised him. Her dream had always been to go to med school.

"We're staying with my mom until I get settled."

"Well, awesome! It's good to have you back." He turned to the teens standing next to him. "Anna, this is my daughter, Sarah, and this is Grady. He's Sean Oakley's son. Sean is the sheriff now and lives next door to us. These two have practically grown up together. Kids, this is Anna Weaver. She went to school with me and your dad. Her mom, Maggie, owns the yarn store downtown."

"And this is my daughter, Ashleigh," Anna said to Sarah and Grady. "I assume you all go to Magnolia Hill High?"

"Yes, ma'am," Sarah replied. "Aren't you in my math and chemistry classes?" his daughter said, turning her attention to Ashleigh. "I really suck at math. It must come so easy to you. You know all the answers when the teacher calls on you."

"It's not that hard once you figure out the rules and concepts," Ashleigh said.

"I wish it was that easy for me," Sarah said.

"So, do you skate?" Grady asked, looking uncomfortable as he pointed at the skateboard on her T-shirt.

"Yeah, I do. Is there a decent skate park in this town?"

Jason smiled. "Kids, why don't you take the food to our seats?" He turned to Anna. "Do you want to join us? I think it would be fun to catch up. Sean should get here soon, too."

"I don't see why not. Ashleigh, can you let Grandma know? Maybe your friends can help you move our stuff while we get more food."

"Of course, Mrs. Weaver," Sarah replied. "We'll take care of it."

They watched them go walk toward the big screen as they stood in line.

"Well, I see the kids are off to a good start." He noticed how her eyes lit up. She was still the same Anna he knew from his youth.

"Ashleigh keeps to herself a lot," she said, more somber now. "Since she became a teenager, she's turned into an alien. It's refreshing to see her talk to other teens again."

"I know what that's like. Sarah hadn't been herself, either," he added. "She isolates herself a lot."

"Ash didn't want to move down here from the city, and I hate having to do this to her in her sophomore year. She hates me right now."

"So what brings you home?" he asked.

"I got divorced. Maggie said you came back to Magnolia Hill ten years ago."

She was divorced. His heart did a somersault in his chest. "Yes. After college, I worked as a meteorologist at the National Weather Service in Atlanta for a while, but I wanted to go back to my roots."

The band began to play again, and the crowd cheered. "We better hurry," he said. They grabbed the new order of nachos and drinks.

"Here they are!" Maggie announced as Jason and Anna approached their seats. "I'm starving!"

"So, Maggie, I have a bone to pick with you. Why didn't you tell me the big news that Anna was coming back to town? You've only been watching Sarah something like a dozen times since spring when I had to work long nights. You didn't mention this to me once."

She shrugged. "You didn't ask me."

Chapter 5

Anna was relieved to see Ashleigh and Grady talk and laugh while Magnolia Hill's mayor gave his speech thanking everyone involved in organizing Family Fun & Movies. Sarah, though, kept her distance. It worried her because she could relate. When life got tough, Anna's first instinct had always been to isolate. She wanted to shut out the world, have her bedroom blinds closed all day, and hope for her problems to go away. It almost never worked. Seeing Sarah sitting in her chair and staring off into the distance made her want to reach out and hug her. It had to be so hard to deal with her mother's death.

Another familiar voice greeting people behind her interrupted her sad thoughts. She twisted in her chair to see if it was him, only talking with a more grown-up voice. A wide grin spread from ear to ear, and she had to restrain herself from jumping up. Instead, she stood up in what she hoped was a measured speed. "Just in time for the movie, Sean," she said.

"Weaver!" he called out. "By God, where have you been hidin'?" he said in his strong southern drawl.

She wasn't sure if it was appropriate to hug her old friend, but he had decided for her. Within seconds of making eye contact, he'd picked her up off her feet and given her a bear hug that nearly knocked the wind out of her lungs.

"Ugh," she managed as she tried to wiggle out of his embrace, then looked at his star. "I can tell you are still as rambunctious as you were in high school. So, you're the sheriff now?" she asked in mock disbelief. "God help the people of this county," she mumbled, teasing him. "I'm kidding! It's great to see you again."

He turned to his friend. "Jason, why didn't you tell me she's in town? We could have arranged an evening with the old gang to hang out at the Sappy Pine."

Jason shrugged. "Man, I only ran into her myself—I mean literally. I agree, though, we need to ask Maggie to see if Anna can come out to play dominoes at the bar."

"Boys, simmer down. I know you all missed me, but I've been busy getting settled and my affairs in order." It was the truth. Hunting after various documents from Colorado to apply for a Georgia paramedic license transfer was quite the ordeal. Then she'd had to get Ashleigh enrolled in school, and Maggie kept her busy at the Spinning Yarns. Tonight was the first time she'd allowed herself to take a breather. She put on a playful grin. "And yes, I'll ask my mom if I can go out with my friends this weekend. I can't make any promises, though."

For a moment, Jason looked excited, then he pouted. "It hurts my feelings that I wasn't at the top of your list to call."

Anna was surprised that the small-town talk hadn't made it to them. "Jenna knew I was here," she said.

"See, exactly my point," Jason replied. "I bet the entire town knew, except for us."

Sean stood with his arms crossed in front of his chest. "Well, it looks like we need to have a talk with Jenna. This is unacceptable! I might have to go get a dozen cupcakes from her bakery in the morning."

"Actually, that's not such a bad idea, Sean," Jason said, playing along. "Saturday morning cupcakes and a nice coffee at her shop..."

"... And a good scolding for keeping secrets," Sean added.

"Oh, stop it!" Anna said, laughing. "She makes some beautiful cupcakes, though, doesn't she?"

"Hey, guys, remember the time when we went storm chasing, and the twister was rain-wrapped?" Sean reminisced. "And the darn thing turned on us. I don't think I've driven that fast since then, not even working in law enforcement." He laughed.

"I do," Anna said. "Somebody screamed like a girl."

"And it wasn't the girls," Jason finished for her.

Yes, they were a crazy bunch. Those were the fun memories, the ones she welcomed.

The light on the silver screen began to flicker, and people scurried to their seats and picnic blankets.

"We're not done, Weaver," Jason whispered in her ear as they took their seats.

She was glad. It was so good to be home and among friends and family. For the first time in years, she felt the genuine love of the people surrounding her.

The feature film was one of the Chronicles of Narnia movies, which was suitable for all ages. She'd seen the movie a hundred times but still enjoyed it. The teens had disappeared to somewhere toward the front of the screen. Anna supposed they'd wanted to escape from the boring adults with all the stories from when they were teenagers in high school.

Halfway through the movies, they ran out of sodas. "Let's do a quick refreshment run," Jason volunteered and touched Anna on the shoulder. "Tag, you're coming with me to help carry the drinks," he said with an impish grin.

She froze when his hand rested a few seconds longer than necessary, afraid that any move would spoil the magic of this moment. Their eyes met. For a moment, she thought a strange force had thrust her back in time, no DeLorean needed.

He held his hand out for her and pulled her out of her chair. "Let's get in line while it's not too crowded," he said.

After, loaded with more chips, candy, and sodas, they were about to head back to join Sean and Maggie when a familiar voice stopped her dead in her tracks. A shudder moved down along her spine.

"Now lookie here, if that's not Fat Anna Banana," a slurred voice taunted from behind her.

Anna cringed and slowly turned into the direction of the insult. It had to be Grace. Out of all the people from her past, she had to run into her childhood nemesis who'd humiliated and bullied her all throughout her school years. Her first instinct was to cower, like when she was a girl. Anger welled up inside her. *No, I will not let her intimidate me again,* she thought. However, no words to fight back would come out of her mouth.

"Cut it out, Grace! You're drunk," Jason said. "Find somebody else to push around."

Grace sneered. "I see you still need a protector, fatty Annie! You're still the weakling you were back then. Nothing has changed. As always, you're running back to that loser of a boyfriend."

"Get lost!" Anna replied and turned away.

Jason whispered into Anna's ear, "Ignore her. She hates not getting the satisfaction of a good fight."

"Well, I hate her," Anna growled.

"Don't let her get to you. She's not worth ruining a wonderful evening like this."

"She's not, Jason!" Humiliated, she handed him her load of food. "I'm sorry, I have to run to the bathroom. Can you carry this to the seats?"

Jason's empathetic expression told her he wasn't buying her fib. He knew her too well. "I've got this. Take all the time you need."

Once Anna locked the door of the porta-potty stall, a silent tear rolled down her cheek. Nothing had changed. Nothing.

* * *

Thinking was dangerous, especially late at night when everyone was already asleep—everyone but her. Like a looping tape, the events of the evening replayed in her mind. As fun as the first half of the evening was, Anna still tasted the bitterness in her mouth. The image of Grace and her venomous words forced itself back into her mind. So much for feeling like home being a good thing. Home. High school. Grace's sharp tongue following her wherever she went.

Anger and shame flared up like a hungry flame that had been dormant for years inside of her. Thoughts of wanting to gauge out the evil woman's eyeballs replaced her moment of happiness that evening. Grace's nasty taunts reminded her she wasn't worthy of anything, be it love or a happy life.

Love. Tonight reminded her of why she couldn't do this again. Grace was right. She didn't deserve love. Jason broke her heart the night of their senior prom and left her crushed. She once thought they would marry after college and have children together. He would be a professional storm chaser, and she would be an MD treating patients in an ER. Together, they would make a great team. Storm chasing was a dangerous hobby, but they both were passionate about it. That bubble burst that Friday night after he took her to the dance. What she thought would be a kiss of strengthened commitment, as they entered a new phase of their lives, turned out to be a kiss goodbye.

She ripped herself from that bad memory. She had no business getting involved with anyone. Not now, her logical mind reminded her. As handsome and fun as Jason was tonight, she had to get her life in order first. For cryin' out loud, she had just gotten out of a bad marriage. Why would he even be interested in her?

Anna smoothed her T-shirt over her belly, ashamed for letting herself go over the years. Jason was famous now, at least in the local area, and he could get any woman he wanted. Just because she had a nostalgic crush on him, and her mind followed that emotion into a rabbit hole, didn't mean he felt the same, or did he? No. They were old friends—friends seeing each other for the first time after decades. That's all. Today she was Weaver, the friend; not Anna, the once love of his life.

The shame of her own perceived rejection fed on her fear of not being good enough to find love and happiness ever again. The emptiness gnawed in her chest and made sitting on her bed unbearable. As if pulled by a force other than her own, she walked down to the kitchen. She rummaged through the freezer until she found that pint of chocolate chip cookie dough ice cream Maggie had bought last week. Anna grabbed a spoon and took it to her room. Maybe the cold treat would fill that giant void in her stomach, and she could forget about her pain.

Food made everything better. She knew that was a lie. Yet, anything that stopped the nagging emptiness inside her, even for a moment, was worth the calories. She took a bite of the cold, soft substance, and in an instant, her taste buds had a party in her mouth. Ah, a chunk of cookie dough! She rolled it to the side of her mouth and bit into the soft mass of sugar, butter, flour, and tiny morsels of chocolate. It was bliss, and her head filled with fireworks. At that moment, nothing else mattered. It was just her and the frozen sensation numbing her mouth, throat, and chest. Then, with the first sign of relief, the pint of ice cream was empty. Reality settled in again. This time, shame and regret surfaced as her gut began to bubble. She should have known better. She did. Yet, she once again had ignored the consequences of her binges that would numb her emotions, this one involving large quantities of dairy.

That dreaded switch flipped on, and everything mattered again. The tape in her head that reminded her she didn't deserve someone like Jason began to play once more, followed by justifications for why she shouldn't be happy.

Chapter 6

A few days after the town's movie event, Ashleigh sat on her bed, baffled, with her phone in her hand. It was still running warm from talking to Sarah for two hours after dinner. She shook her head. "We got nothing done," she said with a sigh. Their plan was to work on a report for their chemistry class, but her notebook still sat unopened on top of her nightstand.

Never in the world did she think she would become friends with one of those proper girls like Sarah. No way! Sarah was the kind of girl who held her straight blond hair out of her face with a headband or clipped it with a cutesy barrette. A skull or some crossbones would have been more Ashleigh's taste. If she didn't know any better, Sarah almost looked like she could be Martha Stewart's daughter, all prim and proper. Ashleigh had always ignored girls like that at her old school. Instead, she hung out with the skater kids whom she could relate to and who didn't take things so seriously.

Judging Sarah had been a big mistake that she now regretted. She felt like a total jerk, especially since that evening at the park. They had hung out at lunch every day since then and threw cold, under-salted fries at each other. Sarah turned out to be fun, and her southern accent added to her quirky personality. Lesson learned— you shouldn't judge people based on their appearance.

Although she and Sarah were polar opposites from each other on the outside, they shared a strong bond that brought them together. It was grief. Ashleigh could so relate to her friend's loss of her mom. She herself was still grieving over getting ripped out of her school and torn away from her friends and her dad. Ashleigh was certain the sadness inside of her would never go away.

She stared at the notebook. With guilt nagging at her, she picked it up and opened it to the next blank page. She knew what the assignment was, but her mind kept wandering, and her pencil kept doodling. When she looked down on the page, she realized she had sketched her old bedroom window with a view of the front range of the Rocky Mountains. In the center stood the majestic snow-capped top of America's Mountain, Pikes Peak.

She missed home. Her room. The skate park. Most of all, she missed her friend Katie. When things got tough at home, she always had her to talk to. Her mom and dad had argued a lot, and she had to admit, her dad got a little rough with her mom sometimes. But she was a daddy's girl through and through. He always treated her like his princess. She wanted to live with him, not her mom, and have her old life back.

Ashleigh tapped the icon to her photo gallery and began to swipe. The newest pictures were of Sarah, Grady, and her making faces at each other at the skate park. She kept swiping until she found the picture of her and Katie as they said goodbye the night before the move.

She had to laugh at their mock sad faces. When her mom got into the car and cranked on the engine, everything changed. That was it. Tears of laughter turned into tears of sadness in the blink of an eye. Both girls had fallen sobbing into each other's arms.

A lone tear trailed down her cheek. Ashleigh wiped it with the back of her hand. Her heart ached for her friend.

As if on cue, her cell buzzed, and she almost dropped it. Ashleigh sat straight on her bed as her friend's picture lit up on the screen. She answered the video call. "Katie!"

"Ash! Where have you been? I was wondering if you'd forgotten about me already."

"Of course not!" Ashleigh laughed. "I've just been busy renovating my room and getting used to this tiny school. It's weird."

"Really? I can't even imagine!" Katie paused then continued. "I miss you, Ashleigh!"

"Oh, I wish I was in Colorado. I swear, I'll never forgive my mom for dragging me down to Podunk, Georgia." Deep inside, she knew that her mom had to do this. It still wasn't fair. And now she was doomed to live here forever, or at least until she was eighteen.

"So how are things down south?" her friend asked.

"Hot and humid all freakin' day. It's just so miserable down here. How do people survive in this climate?" Ashleigh paused. "There's nothing fun to do, and you have to drive forever to the mall."

"That sounds terrible, Ash."

"It is, although I did make some friends in school, but it's not the same as being home."

"So what do you do all day? Ride horses? Feed cows?"

"Not everyone in Georgia has a farm. When I'm not in school or skating, I work at my grandma's craft store."

"Oh, the Ball of Yarn you've been telling me about?"

Ashleigh laughed. "No, silly! It's called Spinning Yarns. This girl from school and I are helping my grandma find craft ideas for teenagers. I've only seen old women come to buy stuff at the shop."

"I can see that."

"We think we can attract younger customers who want to learn how to knit, crochet, and stuff like that, as long as the projects are fun and original. Maybe we could offer classes like the big craft stores do."

"Cool." There was a short lull in their conversation, but Katie broke the silence. "So how's the skating?" she asked.

"They have a nice skate park in town, close to the school. Don't tell my mom, but I kinda like this guy who hangs out there."

"Oh?" Ashleigh watched her friend gasp and come closer to the camera. "Tell me about him!" she whispered.

"His name is Grady. His dad is the sheriff in town. You should see him, he's really cute!" Ashleigh switched to her gallery for a moment and pushed a few buttons. "I just sent you a picture of him." She paused. "Promise me not to tell my mom! She'd have a cow."

"You've got my word."

"Well, besides being totally gorgeous, he seems pretty cool and down to earth." Just being able to talk to someone about her secret crush made her feel better. She could trust Katie. "He has that really cute southern accent. You'd love it!" Even for a country guy, turns out, he wasn't as country as she thought. He didn't fit the stereotype she had imagined guys down south to sound and dress like in her head. Again, Ashleigh, no judging, she admonished herself. "He can also skate like nobody else. There's a skating competition coming up in a few weeks. He asked me to enter."

"Did you?"

"I did. We're practicing every day after school."

"I think I got the picture. Hang on."

She could hear Katie moving around as the video paused.

"Wow, Ash! I'm so jealous. Does Grady have a brother or a cute friend?"

Ashleigh laughed. "You'll have to come to Magnolia Hill. I'm sure we can find you a boyfriend."

"Maybe I will."

"Maybe you should."

For a moment, Ashleigh wondered if Magnolia Hill was really as horrible as she made it out to be.

* * *

Jason checked the latest tropical updates from the National Hurricane Center. Tropical Storm Gerard was strengthening in the Atlantic and tracking toward the southeastern coastal states. Based on the current models, the storm would strengthen to a Category 1 hurricane by tomorrow as it tracked over warm waters. If everything went as predicted, the storm could make landfall anywhere between northern Florida and South Carolina Saturday morning. Bingo! This forecast put Savannah right in the middle of the projected track, which meant he would be extremely busy for the next couple of days.

He leaned back in his office chair, interlaced his fingers behind his head, and stared at the radar loop. Not that he wanted anyone to get hurt—the opposite was true. Witnessing the power of nature fascinated him. When the weather turned violent, he and his friends chased it. Yes, they had a few close calls, but he shrugged these near misses off as extreme adventures gone a tad wrong.

He felt the familiar itch to pack up his gear and meet the about-to-be hurricane head-on. Jason was the only chief meteorologist in the Savannah area who did not mind getting his hair blown about and getting pelted by horizontal rain during catastrophic weather events. His audience even expected him to go into the storms and report from the battlegrounds. He couldn't do it without his trusted team, though. Brandon, one of the station's cameramen, was his loyal companion and made a few cameos on broadcasts as they covered severe weather. His two other staff meteorologists would monitor storm track updates, warnings, and other information in the studio.

Jason turned his office chair toward Brandon, who sat at his desk glued to his monitors editing footage for the next broadcast. "So, Brandon, this hurricane track looks promising."

Brandon, with his shaggy blond hair, turned his head from the monitors with a broad smile. "Are you thinking what I'm thinking?"

"I'm going to the cover Gerard's landfall. Are you with me?" he asked, already knowing the answer.

Brandon now grinned from ear to ear. "Have I ever turned down a chance to stare a hurricane straight in the eye? When are we going?"

"We'll head out Friday morning, when we have a better idea of where Gerard will make landfall."

With one fist raised into the air and a "Yesssss!," Brandon scurried off and left Jason alone with his computer screens.

As he stared at the spaghetti graph in front of him, a memory of Anna and Sean storm chasing with him flashed through his mind. Anna. He couldn't get her out of his head since he saw her last Friday at the park. Ever since, he'd wanted to visit her at the shop. The more he thought about their past, the more he doubted himself. Did Anna want to see him again? He was the one who broke her heart in high school. Talking to her that night felt like old times—the good ones. She had changed little, if at all. Every time their gazes had met, her eyes mesmerized him. She still had that same sense of humor he adored back then. Anna also still appreciated the little things in life that others took for granted, such as the frogs hanging out by the pond providing ambient background music for the film. He hadn't noticed them until she mentioned it. Once she had made him aware of the sound, he couldn't unhear the racket until the movie was over.

An idea struck him. What if he asked Anna to join him on this assignment? Sean would be busy in Magnolia Hill keeping the town safe, but Anna, on the other hand, wasn't working yet. She would have a blast tagging along. Maggie wouldn't mind watching the girls for a night. Not only would this trip give them a chance to catch up in peace, they could also relive their passion for storms again. It was an excellent idea. He pulled out his phone and searched for Spinning Yarns, then dialed the number.

"Spinning Yarns craft shop, how can I help you?" the voice said on the other end of the line.

It was her! His heart skipped a beat, and for a moment, he forgot what he was calling about. "Anna, it's Jason," he began, as he searched for words.

Ah, yes, the storm. He hadn't felt this discombobulated since his first TV broadcast after college, which he'd been sure would cost him his career. That night, he'd been sweating bullets and didn't get a wink of sleep. He'd expected to receive his pink slip first thing in the morning. Thank God, it had happened on a late Sunday show when most viewers slept. The station manager had assured him it would get easier. She was right.

"Hey, listen, we might have to postpone our evening at the Sappy Pine. There's a hurricane coming our way. My cameraman Brandon and I will be covering it from ground zero."

"Oh?" she said at the other end of the line.

Did he hear a hint of disappointment? "Now, wait a minute!" he continued. "I have a better idea. You still like storm chasing, right?"

"I'm listening."

"How about you come with me, you know, just like old times. As friends?"

"Uh, yeah, silly! I'd love to! Colorado had severe weather, but I was always working and didn't have time to go chasing. I think it would be fun," she said, not even attempting to curb her enthusiasm.

His heart did somersaults in his chest. The call was going better than he had expected. "We're heading out Friday morning, and depending on the predicted landfall location, we'll either go to Myrtle Beach, Tybee Island, or

Brunswick, but we'll know more tomorrow."

"What about the girls?"

"Sarah often stays with Maggie or one of my neighbors while I'm on assignment. The girls could have a hurricane slumber party on Friday night."

"I'm sure Mom wouldn't mind. Heck, Sarah and Ashleigh hit it off the other night. They text each other all the time."

"I know," he said. Jason hadn't seen his daughter this upbeat in a long time. "Speaking of hitting it off, I think Ashleigh has a crush on Grady. Don't quote me on that, but I overheard Sarah talking with Ash on the phone last night when they worked on a chemistry assignment."

"Oh, does she?" Anna said. "She told me she was hanging out with him at the skate park to learn new tricks."

The line went silent for a moment. "She's growing up so fast," Anna added, somber. "We got into so much trouble back then when we were her age. Oh my gosh, Jason, you don't think..."

"Relax, Anna." He laughed. "Grady is a good kid."

Anna sighed. "I don't know. If you say so. Ash and I need to talk."

A memory of him kissing her under the bleachers during football practice flashed through his mind. Maybe it was wise to keep this one to himself while they were talking about her daughter. Instead, he steered the conversation into a safer territory. "So, back to Friday," he said. "Remember to pack essentials such as extra clothes, sturdy shoes, a windbreaker. I'll pack a few cases of water, food, and whatever else we might need."

There was a moment of silence. "Can you give Maggie a heads-up? Tell her I'll call her later on tonight when I get home."

"I will."

"Hey," he started before she hung up.

"Yes?"

"I'm really looking forward to this trip!"

"Me, too."

He held his phone in his hand. His gaze fell on the silly background picture of Caroline and Sarah posing for the camera at Okefenokee Swamp Park with alligators in the background. He zoomed in on Caroline's smiling face. Did he make the right decision, inviting Anna on this assignment? They were just friends, he reassured himself. Then he remembered his vows: to love one another until death do us part. To him, it meant until the day he died.

Just friends.

Chapter 7

"I think I have everything we need." Anna checked her backpack one more time and made sure she brought her charger cable for her cell and two spare battery packs. Next, she zipped her medical supply bag that she always kept in the trunk of her car in case she drove by a wreck. It had come in handy more than once. Now that she was about to head into a potential disaster area, bringing her emergency gear was a no-brainer. Last night, she'd made an extra trip to the drugstore to grab a few more packs of gauze, bandages, distilled water, and hydrogen peroxide. She was ready to rock 'n' roll.

"Not quite." Maggie handed her a cooler. "Here. I made sandwiches, boiled eggs, and some other goodies that should keep. I doubt any restaurants will be open on Tybee because of the mandatory evacuation, but I wanted to make sure you three won't starve."

"Thanks, Mom," Anna said as she put down the cooler and zipped up the medic bag.

"I know how much you like this weather stuff. So, promise me you and Jason have fun! And most important, be careful! I always worry when you go out storm chasing." Maggie rested her hand on her shoulder, then continued, somber. "Anna, Jason is a wonderful man and dad. He's nothing like Luke."

She couldn't believe her mother. What was it with her? Did she have psychic powers or mind reading skills? "Mom, we're not dating! We're going as friends. Plus, the ink on my divorce papers hasn't even dried yet. I have plenty of other things to worry about, like..." She paused. "Like getting my new life together. There's really no time for a relationship."

"Baby girl, you've already made that clear. I just wanted you to understand that Jason would never lay a hand on you." She squeezed Anna's shoulder and put her warm hand on her cheek. "I'll leave it at that, okay?" She patted her cheek for good measure, then walked back to the kitchen counter to put away the extra sandwich fixings.

Anna saw Jason's truck pull up in the driveway. "He's here," she called out. "I've gotta go!"

Jason opened the screen door and let himself in. "Good morning, ladies," he said with a smile capable of making all the eligible women in Liberty County swoon.

He looked stunning with his station polo tucked into his jeans. His ball cap with the same logo gave him more of the impish look that she had missed all these years.

"My, you are handsome today," Maggie said with one hand on her waist.

"Why, thank you, Maggie. You're quite beautiful this morning, too," he replied and kissed her on the forehead.

Maggie waved him off. "Oh, stop it,"

she said, her cheeks turning a soft pink. "You kids better head out."

He walked over to Anna and kissed her the same way. "Hi," he whispered, barely audible.

Anna giggled. "Hi, Jason!" she said. "Stop making Mom blush and grab a bag."

He lifted her jam-packed rucksack over his shoulder as if it didn't have any weight to it. Next, he grabbed her medic bag. "Smart move," he said, lifting the bag. "You don't know how many times I've been out in the field wishing I had more than my first aid kit in the truck."

"Well," Anna said. "It gets better. You have your own personal paramedic accompanying you on this adventure."

Maggie shook her head. "You two make me worry myself to death!"

"Sorry, Mom," Anna said. "We'll be careful."

"That's what you said last time."

"But, Maggie," Jason said with his charming southern drawl. "We were careful that time. It was the tornado that didn't behave that day."

Maggie threw her hands up in desperation. "You kids are too much for me! Just go before I fall to pieces."

Jason turned around one more time as he opened the screen door. "Awww, Maggie, we are pros at this. And thank you again for letting Sarah spend the night. We'll call you later on when we get to the hotel," he assured her. "You should be okay weather-wise. As of the current forecast, you should only get a few inches of rain. Maybe you'll see a thunderstorm or two with some of the stronger rainbands. The hurricane will downgrade as soon as it makes landfall and then make a sharp turn northward, so you should be safe. Remember to keep an eye on the news and evacuate if you need to, okay?"

Maggie nodded. "Got it. I've been living here for longer than you've been alive. We got this! Now go!"

"I love you, Mom," Anna said, lugging the rest of her stuff out of the house.

Anna enjoyed the ride with Jason to Tybee Island. If she didn't know any better, she never would've guessed that a Category 1 hurricane was aiming right at them. The sky was blue, with only a slight breeze gently swaying the leaves on the trees. By this time tomorrow, holy hell would break loose, and they'd be lucky if the trees had any leaves left.

Every once in a while, she sneaked a peek at Jason as he negotiated traffic, hoping he would be too busy to notice. His sunglasses made him look even more appealing, and it was hard for her to unglue her gaze from him. Just friends, she reminded herself. Just friends. She felt light and giddy inside. This was going to be an awesome weekend. Content, Anna looked forward to what lay ahead of them. She relaxed into her seat, enjoying the ride.

They navigated through the Savannah traffic. Once they made it through the worst stretch, the city scape transformed into marshland. "Amazing!"

Jason smiled, and for a moment, their eyes met. He held her gaze, but she looked away. Friends.

She noticed that the traffic heading away from the islands was thick, but only a handful of vehicles were traveling toward the incoming disaster. At least these people were smart and heeding the evacuation order. Anna knew that what they were doing was dangerous, but she trusted Jason with her life. He wouldn't let anyone get hurt in the storm. They'd done this since they were teens, and he had made his passion his profession. What could go wrong?

She rolled the window down. "Ah, I've missed the ocean," she said, closing her eyes and taking in the salty sea air filling the cab of the truck. "Remember when we used to go to Tybee almost every weekend in the summer?"

"...and almost every time, the afternoon thunderstorms would move in, leaving the beach deserted after the rain."

"That's the best time to hang out at the shore," Anna replied. "After the tourists have gone back to their hotels and to get ready for dinner."

The left corner of Jason's mouth turned up into a cheeky smile.

"What?" Anna asked.

"Oh, nothing. I just thought of the time when we were swimming in the rain one summer." His grin broadened. "I have to confess, that swim was visually stunning."

Anna blushed. Her bikini top had come untied in the powerful waves and he'd gotten a full view before she'd realized what had happened. "Yeah, I remember," she said. "Not funny!"

"What?" he asked. "It was my happiest memory at the beach."

She punched him in the arm. "Of course it was."

"Speaking of the beach, Brandon will meet us at the hotel in about an hour," Jason said as they were cruising through Thunderbolt Island. "He's already there with Bessie, our weather van, recording footage and scoping out good views for the broadcasts."

"I'm assuming he's gone chasing with you before?" she asked.

"Brandon? Oh yeah! He's been out there with me covering every major weather event. He's just as nutty as I am when it comes to weather, except he knows how to capture these things on camera better than anybody I know."

"I can't wait to meet him," she said, then filled her lungs with more of the precious sea air. It'd been so long. Her goal was to soak in every single moment of this chase and commit it to memory with all her senses. This would be a trip to remember.

They passed several more police barriers along the way, another warning to turn around immediately, which they ignored.

* * *

It was five minutes until noon. Anna watched Jason insert his earpiece into his ear to communicate with the studio. Brandon adjusted his camera tripod to capture the already violent surf thrashing against the long boardwalk.

She was excited to see Jason live in action, doing what he did best–talking about weather and sharing his passion with the world, or at least with the people of Savannah and surrounding areas. A thought crossed her mind, and a small snicker escaped her. Tomorrow, Jason and Brandon would be those crazy weathermen on TV she'd always made fun of—the ones struggling to give their reports during hurricanes and fighting to stay upright. When she realized she was just as crazy for coming with him, she shook her head and walked closer to the pier for some shade.

Anna's gaze traveled to the horizon out at sea, but most of the clouds were still far away. Knowing that soon they would get hit by a Category 1 hurricane made her giddy. At the same time, she was terrified. Anna struggled to imagine the impact Gerard could have on them. They'd had some violent hailstorms, blizzards, and flash floods in Colorado that required rescues, but a hurricane was a few levels up in magnitude. She turned to look at the hotels and condos lining the beach. Would they hold up against the storm? She prayed to God they did. For now, she only wanted to enjoy the view—the view of Jason. Just friends, the annoying voice inside of her head kept saying, interrupting her daydreaming.

Brandon counted off the seconds on his hand.

"Hello, folks, Chief Meteorologist Jason Morrison here, reporting from Tybee Island. What you see is the calm before the storm. Gerard is now a strong Category 1 hurricane still spinning in the Atlantic and is expected to make landfall right here tomorrow morning around eight a.m. A mandatory evacuation order is still in effect for the nearby coastlines. For what to expect, and more on tomorrow's timeline, stay tuned for details during our weather segment in a few minutes."

Jason winked at her, then returned his focus to his work.

Her heart fluttered in response. This would be an interesting weekend. The storm hadn't even arrived yet. She watched the guys get ready for the main weather segment while she enjoyed the sea breeze cooling off her hot skin. Dang, her sunscreen was still in the truck. *I can tough it out a few more minutes,* she thought. Her shoulders had already turned a little pink. Even though Colorado had more sunny days than rain, her skin wasn't used to the sun anymore.

Once she had arrived in Georgia, it took less than a day to revert to tank tops, shorts, and flip-flops. She wasn't used to showing this much skin. There was no need to in Colorado. The weather in the Deep South was another story. The hot, damp air made her clothes stick to her like a wet rag within minutes of leaving the house. She soon realized that wearing weather-appropriate clothing outweighed worrying about her imperfections.

At first, she had tucked and pulled on her shorts to cover up her thighs, but the last hint of her inhibitions evaporated when she entered the grocery store the day after they had arrived. She had no words to describe the fashion choices. "Stop taking pictures, Ash!" she had hissed at her daughter, which earned her an eye roll. "And don't you dare put anything on Snapchat!"

The broadcast was over in no time. Anna joined the men as they broke down the equipment. Brandon had parked Bessie next to a boarded-up souvenir shop. They stashed everything inside, and Jason slammed the door shut. "Hey, Brandon?"

"Yeah?"

"We'll walk back to the hotel from here. I'll come and get you around three so we can prep for the evening broadcast."

Brandon gave them a thumbs-up and left.

They strolled back to the beach, not too close to where the waves broke, though. Anna's legs dragged through the dry sand that gave with every step. She knew she'd be sore in the morning if they continued to walk like this for a while.

"Are you sure Brandon is okay?" she asked, somewhat guilty that she was taking Jason away from their usual routines.

"He's fine. As long as you give him cable TV to watch, internet access, and time to text with his girlfriend, he'll be good to go."

"Did she not want to come?"

Jason shook his head. "Nah, she works in the hotel business. With all these evacuees, her manager makes her work when weather is coming."

"That makes sense." Anna watched the waves crash against the pier. Experiencing the brute force of the sea gave her goose bumps. She noted that some brave souls stood at the end of the outlook point and backed away as spray hit them. "Those people are insane!" she said. "All it takes is a rogue wave to wash them into the sea. Good luck to them to make it back to land before they get slammed into a rock or the pier beams."

"They know," he said, wrapping his arm around her shoulder. "They want to take the risk, regardless of rules or warnings."

Warm fuzzies spread from where his arm touched her. She rested her head against his shoulder and closed her eyes. Anna couldn't even remember when she last shared a moment like this with Luke. It didn't matter. Luke was history. Right now was all that counted. The friendship between her and Jason was wonderful and real. That's what she needed—a good friend.

Keep telling yourself that, the voice in her head told her. She wished it would just shut up.

They stopped and looked out to sea. Even though the wall of clouds was still distant, it was closing in on them. Only the breeze picked up slightly. The sky above them was still blue, and the seagulls swooped around them, hoping for a piece of bread or a potato chip to snatch.

Walking on the beach felt like home again. Walking on the beach with Jason made it feel even better. It was right. But she had to remind herself that they were friends. Friends that liked each other. A lot. Her common sense wanted her to wriggle out from under his arm, but she couldn't bring herself to do it. She didn't want to. All she wanted was to hang on that moment just a little while longer.

Jason started moving again. "Look, a sand dollar!" He let go of her and picked it up. "It's still intact," he said and held it out to her.

She took the white shell and brushed the sand off with one finger. "I still have the one you gave me last time we were on this beach. Mom never cleaned out my room." She laughed. "I found all kinds of stuff I had forgotten about. Remember that cheesy science trophy I got? Mom never tossed that thing."

"You were always the smart one between the two of us. What happened with med school?"

"Well, I was in my junior year in college when Luke and I got married. He was majoring in criminal justice and graduated that year. Right after, he went to the police academy, and then he took a job in Colorado Springs. We figured I could continue school in Colorado, but we were tight on money, so I went to a community college to get my paramedic degree instead. I never picked up the books again once I started working those crazy shifts."

"Are you happy?" he asked.

"You know, I am. I love helping people. Even though the shifts are long, the work is hard, and the pay is crap, it's incredibly rewarding."

He tucked her closer to him. "I'm glad you like it. You must have a calling to do this kind of work."

"It's tough, mind you," she said. "You see lots of tragic accidents. The ones involving kids or innocent crime victims are very hard to deal with, but you have to get past those calls. Some of them hit hard and stick with you…"

Jason turned to her. His gentle smile was replaced with an expression of concern. "Wanna tell me about it?"

She was tempted to open up to him and tell him how one New Year's Eve call started the horrific chain reaction of events that ultimately brought her back home to Magnolia Hill. Instead, Anna shook her head. "Maybe another time." She didn't want to dwell on this part of her past anymore, not when she was here with Jason, waiting for a hurricane to come. "Let's not talk about my train wreck of a life," she said, changing the topic. "We have a hurricane on our hands!" She twisted out of his embrace, kicked some sand at his legs, and ran. "Catch me if you can!"

Jason took off after her. "Oh no, you didn't just mess up my broadcast jeans, Weaver!"

She turned around and ran backward for a few steps. "Remember, I also ran cross-country!"

"So? I played football!"

When he got closer, she turned again and ran through the hot sand. Her thighs ached, and her lungs hurt, but she gave it all she had. "What's the matter, Morrison? Did being a weatherman make you soft?" she taunted him.

"That's it!" he yelled. "I'm coming for you now!"

Anna had no idea where he got a final burst of speed, but he caught up to her with a few long steps and tackled her. "Ooooh!" At least they landed on the sand and not on concrete. Anna felt something digging into her back. "Ouch, ouch, ouch!"

Jason eased himself off her and rolled onto the side. "Are you okay? Did I hurt you?" he said, breathing hard.

Anna rolled the other way and dug out a pointy seashell from under her back and laughed. "You could have punctured my left lung with this shell. That hurt!"

"Roll over and let me see."

She turned onto her belly, and he lifted her shirt a few inches to check on her wound. "Yep, I can confirm, using my meteorological judgment, that you're almost bleeding," he said, then lowered her shirt again.

She rolled onto her side and propped her head up on her hand. "I wish the sea was calmer so we could go for a swim," she said.

"Me too." He wiped his hand on his jeans, then tried to clean the sand off her forehead. "You do need a shower, though."

Their eyes locked for a moment, and his cell phone rang. He let out a mild curse and helped Anna onto her feet before answering.

"Hello?" Jason stared at the hurricane churning in the Atlantic in front of them. "It's strengthened?" He paused. "Okay, I'll go to the van and check the new data. Thanks for the heads-up. I'll call you back in a few."

"Work?" Anna asked after he hung up.

"Yep. The Hurricane Hunter report just came in. It looks like we have a Category 2 coming at us now. I'm sorry, Anna, I have to do some work. Let me walk you to the hotel, so you can shower and take a break. I'll come by your room when I get a minute, okay?" He brushed a layer of sand off her cheek and kissed her on it. "Hmmm, salty. I think I just kissed a mermaid."

Chapter 8

Jason grabbed his laptop from the room and walked to the storm tracker vehicle. He fired up the computers and got his team at the station on a video call. He could tell with the new data that Gerard's eyewall had tightened since the last report, another indicator the hurricane was strengthening.

"Hurricane Hunter reports clocking wind speeds at ninety-eight miles per hour during their last flight. Gerard has slowed down quite a bit," Mark, one of his meteorologists, said. "We're now talking a higher rain impact than we expected as the storm moves inland, maybe two to three additional inches."

"That's not good. What's the current prediction for landfall?"

"Well, Jason, stay where you're at. Gerard will make landfall on Tybee Island as a strong Cat 2 tomorrow morning, right around eight thirty a.m."

Jason threw his fist in the air. "Yes!" This meant by tomorrow, he would be right in the middle of the action. He hoped he'd picked a hotel sturdy enough to withstand the hurricane-force winds. He'd learned the hard way one summer that hotel choice was a major factor in staying safe during weather events like this. That summer, while covering another hurricane, he'd found himself roofless on the second floor of a motel. He would not make that mistake again.

"When can I tell the boss we're going live?" Mark asked.

"Give us about fifteen minutes to get situated. I'll let you know when we're ready."

As soon as the video call ended, Jason hurried up the hotel stairs to get Brandon from his room. Turns out, Brandon was already on top of it.

"Hey, Jason, I'm glad I found you," Brandon said, running down the stairs, holding up his cell. "I got a text from one of my videographer buddies working for the Weather Channel. Gerard is a Cat 2 now."

"Yes, I already checked the new data. Can you get your camera ready for a broadcast? I told Mark we should be ready to go live in fifteen minutes." He checked his watch. "Make that ten."

His friend cocked his head. "Um, and you also might want to wash the sand off your face before we go live. You look like you've been romping around on the beach."

Jason felt the grit when he wiped his forehead. "I tripped."

Brandon laughed. "Yeah, I don't believe you, but if that's what you want to call it..."

He smirked at his friend. "Go set up your equipment on the beach and I'll meet you down there in a minute."

"Okay, boss."

"Five minutes max!" Jason held up five fingers as he ran up the last flight of stairs.

The cool water on his face was refreshing after coming in from the sticky sea air. He patted his face dry with a small towel and noticed his wedding band on his hand in his reflection. Caroline. A stab of guilt coursed through his body. He was having such a great time with Anna that he had forgotten about Caroline. We're here only as friends, he had to remind himself. What was he doing getting all goo-goo-eyed and kissy at Anna? Why did he even bring her? He had promised Caroline that he'd always love her. In his mind, that meant even after death. Why did he want to torture himself by bringing Anna? He knew dang well that he'd once loved her, and to be honest, he still did.

His wedding band, which he still wore on his left ring finger, even after her death, was suddenly bulkier and heavier than before. It was something he held on to, something that reminded him every day of the love he had lost. He had vowed to her to love her until the day he died, but she was taken from him first. He missed having his wife around, someone to talk to and be with, do family stuff with. Every moment he got to spent with her had been a gift.

He was grateful for her giving him such a wonderful daughter who he adored from the moment Caroline had told him about her pregnancy. He was grateful for her when she'd still allowed him to pursue his passion of storm chasing with Brandon, even when he came home with a hail battered truck or holes in the windshield.

Anna was a friend, and that was how it would stay. What had he expected? Anna's return to Magnolia Hill didn't mean she returned to him. Both their lives had changed in the last twenty years. Now was not the time to rush into something he couldn't give his full heart to. Maybe one day he would be ready for a new relationship, but not now. The wounds were still too fresh.

He put on a clean polo, headed down to the beach, and texted Anna that he'd be busy with the broadcast and that she could join them, only if she wanted.

* * *

Anna watched Jason and Brandon set up for the broadcast, sitting on the beach a short distance away from them. Something wasn't right, though. She noticed that he acted more distant before going on air, as if something was bothering him. Maybe he had received bad news about the hurricane. She'd ask him when they wrapped up this show and he had a minute.

The roar of the crashing waves made it difficult to hear Jason talk. Instead of moving closer and getting in their way, she stretched out her legs in the sand, closed her eyes, and leaned her head back. The breeze felt wonderful on her warm skin.

Anna smiled at the sound of the screeching seagulls. When she used to ride to Tybee with her friends on the weekends, it never failed that at least one group of tourists thought it would be cute to feed the birds. As a result, a giant flock of seagulls would hover over and dive-bomb them. Amateurs. *Never feed the seagulls,* she thought. At least it was entertaining to watch them deal with the attacks.

Her phone buzzed, and Anna checked the screen.

Are you enjoying the beach? her mom's text read.

Loving it, she replied.

Are you with Jason? The news said he'll be on after the commercials.

Yeah, I'm watching him and his camera man get ready to go live, she typed.

Ash & Sarah just got in the door. We're at the shop. They look like they're up to something, Maggie replied.

The corners of Anna's mouth lifted to a smile. *I'm sure whatever it is, you can handle it. Tell Ash hi. We'll call later.*

She dropped the phone into her lap and closed her eyes again. The shop had always been a healing place for the Weaver women. For Maggie, it had been a way to cope with being a single parent and, at the same time, to make a living. Watching Ash immersed in small projects at the shop since their arrival gave her hope her daughter would also adjust to her new surroundings in time. For Anna, helping her mom in the shop was the break she desperately needed from it all. She needed to heal from the abusive relationship, the trauma she'd seen as a paramedic, and she needed a break from the move. The Spinning Yarns shop was a place where she could think things through in peace. Mundane and relaxing tasks, such as painting window frames, wiping down shelves, and sorting colors of yarn allowed her to let her thoughts flow. There was something Zen about that line of work. Peace was what she needed right now—peace, like this calm before the storm.

A light wind gust tugged on her ponytail. She opened her eyes. The clouds in the distance looked daunting. Anna saw the defined edge to the monster of a storm. The closer Gerard moved toward them, the more excited she became. Not that she wanted to see things destroyed or lives lost, but witnessing the power of nature first-hand gave her an adrenaline rush like no other. Unlike Jason, though, she didn't care so much about the science behind it. She just wanted to be there.

Jason adjusted his ballcap, and his posture straightened—a sign she assumed he was about to go on air.

Anna stood and walked closer to hear Jason better.

He smiled and winked at her, then focused on the camera.

"Folks, if you're just tuning in, Gerard is now a Category 2 hurricane with sustained winds of one hundred and two miles per hour. To give you a perspective, these winds can do major damage to mobile homes, roofs and other structures. The rains might cause flooding in low-lying and flood-prone areas..." he said, then went on to describe the current conditions and how they would change overnight. "Stay safe, everyone! Keep your TV on this channel for updates about Hurricane Gerard and listen to your local law enforcement. This storm is a humdinger!" Jason told his audience. "I will see you back with the latest from Tybee Island as conditions change."

Brandon turned off the camera and started breaking down the equipment.

Anna walked over to Jason. "Well, Mr. Weatherman, the Savannah region is in good hands," she said.

He nodded, but she sensed something still wasn't right. "I'm worried about this one, Anna. It looks like the storm will almost be a Cat 3 by the time it makes landfall. Let's call home to make sure Maggie is aware." He put his cell on speaker.

"Oh, she was watching all right," Anna said.

"Hi, kids," Maggie answered her phone.

"Hi, Maggie," Jason said.

"I'm here, too, Mom," Anna added.

A muffled voice called out, "Girls, your mom and dad are on the phone!" She turned her attention back to them. "Let me put you on speaker too, so the kids can listen in. How do you turn this darn speaker on?" Maggie mumbled. Anna could hear her messing with the phone.

"Here, Grandma," Ash said. "You just push this speaker button on your keypad."

Anna smiled at Jason. "Bless her heart," she mouthed.

"Okay, kids, I think it's working now," Maggie said, louder than usual.

"We can hear you just fine," Jason said. "Have you been watching the news?"

"Of course, darling," Maggie said. "We'll be fine. My house sits high enough, so flooding shouldn't be an issue."

"I'm still ninety percent sure that the storm will turn north as it makes landfall," Jason added. "But remember, those outer bands can still be powerful and destructive and cover a wider area.”

“Don’t worry about us, honey. I have fresh batteries in the weather radio, and I did another trip to the store for more supplies while the kids were in school. You won’t believe how empty the shelves were. Like I said, we’re ready.”

“Thanks again, Maggie, for watching Sarah. Don’t be afraid to ask her for help with anything. Speaking of Sarah, how is she?” Jason asked.

“Well, I’m sure she can tell you all about it. Here ya go, baby girl. Talk to your father.”

“Hey, Dad.”

“Hey, sweetie. Are you girls getting along?” he asked.

She giggled. “Of course, Dad. We’re designing a new friendship bracelet.

Ashleigh is really good at that stuff. We want to make statement bracelets, kinda like friendship bracelets with words. Maggie is letting us use some of the yarn at the shop."

"That's awesome! You could make a few and sell them on consignment in the store if they turn out," Anna added.

"Yeah! That's the plan," Ashleigh said.

"We were also thinking of teaching a class if there's interest. Maggie is all for it," Sarah said. "Ashleigh is making a cool skater bracelet for Grady right now. She designed the pattern at school today."

"Sarah!" Ashleigh hissed in the background.

"No really, Mrs. Weaver," she continued. "It's super cool!"

"Well, I can't wait to see it." Anna couldn't be any happier about the girls getting along so well. Ashleigh was coming out of her shell. Moving home had been a good decision, so far.

"Girls," Jason said. "The hurricane is strengthening, so I need you to listen to Maggie, especially if you have to evacuate. You got that?"

"Yes, Dad."

"Oh, I forgot to tell you, Anna," Maggie said. "Sean is dropping Grady off at the house later on while he's working during the storm, too."

Anna was about to say something, but Maggie beat her to it.

"I know what you're thinking, and yes, the kids will be supervised at all times. Doors stay open and all that stuff. Most likely, Grady will spend the night, but we've already worked things out. He'll sleep on the couch downstairs, and the girls will share Ashleigh's room. I've already discussed the rules with them, and they will hear them again when Grady gets here."

She heard a groan from the girls in the background and suppressed a smile. "Mom, just know that kids these days are creative."

"Like you? I remember you sneaking out of the window late at night to see Jason."

"You do?"

"No, not really, but I guess you just told on yourself." She laughed. "Kidding aside, the kids will be fine. Don't worry about them. Okay?"

"Okay, Mom. Love you."

They ended the call. "What do you say we grab dinner early?" Jason suggested. "The greasy spoon across the street looks like it's still open for business. Let's go before they shut down for the weather. Are you coming, Brandon?"

"I'm starving," Brandon said, rubbing his belly.

Anna and Jason helped Brandon to put the equipment into the van, then the trio headed across the street to see about something to eat.

Indeed, the restaurant still served food. The owner had boarded up the windows and rigged the open sign so it was visible from the street.

"I'll be open as long as we have power," the owner had told them. He had no intention of evacuating. "Plus, someone has to feed these reporters," he'd added. "What can I get you?"

"I will take a Bushwacker cocktail." She examined the short menu for a second. "And for dinner, I'll have the fish and chips."

"How about you, sir. Hey, aren't you the weather guy?"

Jason nodded. "Yes, I am."

"I watch the Weather Channel all the time," he added, "especially when we got storms like this comin'."

Jason's face dropped in disappointment.

"Did I say something wrong?" the man asked.

She giggled. Poor Jason almost got to enjoy his moment of fame. Almost. The man looked so excited to see someone famous, she didn't have the heart to correct him.

"No, sir, but I work for a local station."

A lightbulb went on. "Oh, sorry, my mistake. You're the chief weatherman. I knew I'd seen you somewhere!"

"That's okay. It happens all the time," Jason grumbled and returned his attention to the menu. "Well, I'll order the fried chicken with mashed potatoes, gravy, and coleslaw. I'll pass on the alcoholic beverage. I'm still working," he explained.

"I'll take my dinner to go," Brandon said as he ordered his meal.

"Don't be silly. You are not interrupting anything," Anna insisted, but she understood if he didn't feel comfortable around them catching up.

Their food came fairly quickly, maybe because they were about the only customers left.

"Thanks, man," Brandon said to the waiter, then grabbed his box and pushed his now empty chair toward the table. "I'm sorry for not sticking around, but my girl is waiting for me to call." He gave a peace sign with his free hand and walked out of the restaurant.

"I really feel bad for him wanting to leave," Anna said as she squirted some ketchup on her fries.

"Nah, don't worry about it. He likes to hang out in his room and watch TV, even if it's just us two on assignment."

"If you say so." Anna enjoyed every bite of her meal. She didn't realize how hungry she was. It was the sea air, or at least that's what people said. Maybe it was all the running she did on the beach today. Heck, even just walking on the sand was tiring. No wonder she wanted to eat every morsel of food on her plate. Her thoughts drifted to the tender moment they had shared earlier on the beach. She still remembered the tingle on her skin from when he had wiped the sand away off her forehead and kissed her. He hadn't changed at all. He was still the same Jason she'd known in high school, a romantic and a genuine soul. The sound of Jason pushing his plate away pulled her back to reality.

"I needed that," he said with a smile and patted his belly. "Are you okay, Anna?"

"Yes, I'm fine." She took one last sip of her frozen drink until her straw made a gurgling sound. "These things are yummy! They taste like a chocolate milkshake. So—" She took a sharp inhale. Uh-oh! The pain in her throat spread toward her sinuses. She pinched the bridge of her nose. "Ouch!"

"Too fast?" he asked, one corner of his mouth turning upward toward the laugh lines around his eyes.

She nodded. "I'm glad you think it's funny," she managed between the throbbing pain.

"Well, it is. Listen, Anna," he began, his face more serious now. "Look, I've been meaning to tell you this for a long time. I'm sorry about how things ended with us in high school. I knew that I'd only be coming home from Oklahoma for the holidays. You deserved someone that could spend time with you."

"It could've worked," Anna said. "We both would've been busy with schoolwork, and before you knew it, time would've passed, and we could've spent the holidays together at home."

He shook his head. "No, Anna, it couldn't have worked. It wouldn't have been fair to you to wait six years to get my master's. Think about it. Long distance relationships don't work over such a period of time."

"I could've transferred to Oklahoma."

"Your scholarships were for Georgia universities."

"So? We could've found a way to make it work," she said.

"It's not that easy. You would've been an out-of-state resident. Tuition would've been double. I had scholarships and grants from the university to get me through most of my education. Mind you, I also had a lot of student loan debt to pay off for years after I graduated."

Her heart sank. He was right. She couldn't have afforded out-of-state tuition, even if she would've started at a community college. "We could've married, and I could've waited a year to start college to meet state residency requirements."

He shook his head. "Oh, Anna. We were so young then," he said, his voice soft.

"You should have at least given me the choice instead of just breaking up with me."

Jason cupped his hand over hers. His skin was soft and warm to the touch. "I'm so sorry I hurt you, Anna," he said. "This is not an excuse, by any means, but I strongly believed I was doing the right thing back then. All I wanted was to give you a chance to move on with your life instead of us both being miserable waiting for the next letter, the next call, and the next holiday. There was nothing more I wanted than spend the rest of my life with you. You meant the world to me, but in my immature mind, the most logical thing to do was end our relationship, knowing it would be painful for both of us, but in the long run it would be for the best. That way we could concentrate on school and do well in our careers, with the hope that one day, we would meet again."

Anna fought the tears that were blurring her vision. "It would have been okay, Jason. I loved you so much, and you broke my heart."

"I'm sorry, Anna."

She blinked a few more times, slowly pulled her hand out from under his, and tried to smile. She didn't want to embarrass herself in front of Jason by reliving the dark period in her life any more than she just did, and had so many times throughout the years. Instead, she tried to steer the topic elsewhere. "So tell me about your wife.

How did you meet?" As soon as the words left her lips, she regretted opening her mouth. *Great, as if that topic is less depressing,* she thought.

Jason's gaze softened. "We met at a chili cook-off after I graduated from college. She was amazing, and I wish you could have met her. We were married a year later. Shortly after, we moved to Atlanta, where I worked for the National Weather Service for five years. She enjoyed living in the city, but Atlanta was too much for her. I lucked out when a meteorologist position opened up at my current TV station. Caroline was ready to escape that crazy city, and Savannah was still big enough to satisfy the city girl in her. Sarah was born a few months after we moved to Magnolia Hill."

"She sounds like she was a wonderful woman," Anna said.

"She was." He took a moment to gather himself. "She was killed by a drunk driver after picking up Sarah from a friend's house. We didn't even get to say goodbye." Jason looked down. "Sean was at the scene after it happened. He said by the time they got there, she was already gone."

"I'm sorry," Anna said. She didn't know what else to say. She watched his eyes tear up, and this time, she reached out to him.

He accepted her hand and stroked it with his thumb. "It still hurts."

Chapter 9

Anna found a comfortable spot on the beach close to where Brandon and Jason were about to do their 10 p.m. broadcast. Brandon had shone a light toward the dock so viewers could see the violent waves battering the pier. In her opinion, they were a little close to the water, but it was their call. The ominous clouds out at sea continued to close in on them. The wind had picked up considerably, but not anywhere near to hurricane level yet. She watched the lightning illuminate the sky in a spiderweb pattern in the distance. Gerard was on his way. There was no stopping the impending disaster.

She couldn't make out anything Jason said over the roar of the sea. Instead, she thought about the dinner earlier that evening and their conversation. Her heart went out to him and Sarah. She had seen many drunk driving accidents in her line of work, and most ended in tragedy. She watched Jason. He wasn't wearing his ball cap this time, and his semi-short hair was blowing in the wind as the spotlight shone on him. Was she the only one about to swoon?

Brandon lowered his camera. "That's a wrap. Let's call it a night," he said and carried his gear to the weather van. The last thing he did was turn off his light. "I'll meet you two in the hotel lobby in the morning," Brandon shouted.

"Okay," Jason called back. "I'll get you up at five. We'll have a busy day ahead of us."

Brandon slammed the van door shut and waved one more time out of the window as he drove off to the hotel.

They were alone again. Jason walked over to her, and together, they strolled along the beach. "It's hard to believe that we have a strong Cat 2 hurricane on our doorstep," she said. "The lightning is beautiful out here." She stopped, then looked up at him, barely able to make out his facial features in the darkness. "Do you think we'll be safe tomorrow?"

"I hope so," he whispered. "I picked the sturdiest hotel on the island, and it's far enough from the water to keep us away from the storm surge."

"Will you rescue me if Gerard carries me away?" she asked with a tempting smile as if to bait him.

"I promise to run after you and catch you by the foot."

She giggled and cuddled up to him. She could tell that he hesitated, but then he wrapped his arm around her shoulder again. Together they stood on the beach watching Mother Nature's light display in the darkness, the thunderous soundtrack of the waves breaking only yards in front of them.

If it were up to her, she would stay with him on the beach all night long awaiting Gerard.

"Isn't it amazing?" he said in a soft voice, just loud enough for her to hear over the crashing waves in front of them.

"It is." She snuggled a little more into his shoulder, and he tightened his embrace.

The lightning struck closer now.

"I hate to end this moment," Jason said, "but we need to get ready for the morning. The first rainband should arrive in less than an hour. It'll be downhill from there."

"Just another minute or two?" she asked, hoping to buy more time in his arms.

He gave her a squeeze and kissed her on her head. "Okay, I think we can manage that."

She couldn't remember the last time she'd shared a moment like this with anyone other than Jason. She didn't want it to end. Even though she knew she shouldn't get romantically involved with anyone until she'd gotten some normalcy back in her life, she couldn't make herself break the spell that bound them.

Anna was hyperaware of her surroundings and tried to soak in every moment with Jason so she could commit it to memory. The sound of the waves, the salty air, and the sand filling the spaces between her toes with each step filled her senses. Best of all was being close to Jason again. Oh, how she'd missed that feeling.

Suddenly, a sharp pain in her toe made her stop in her tracks. "Aaaagh, dang it!"

Jason steadied her. "Whoa, what's the matter?"

"I stubbed my toe." She looked down and saw a big piece of coral sticking out from the sand. Anna lifted her foot closer to where she could see, then ripped her flip-flop off. "Dang it, that hurts!" As she yanked her foot closer, she realized that the sharp edges of the coral had sliced her toe right open. She had a bunch more cuss words in store but opted in favor of just sucking it up and letting the waves of pain pulse for a moment.

"What can I do?" Jason asked, still holding her up by her arm.

"Can you grab that flip-flop for me? I might also need help getting to your truck. My medic bag is still on the back seat." Her toe throbbed like the dickens. She stared at the what now seemed a very long distance to the parking lot, considering her unfortunate circumstance. She groaned at the task ahead of her.

Without warning, Jason swooped her over his shoulder and carried her fireman-style.

"Waaaah! What are you doing?" she called out as he carried her through the sand to his truck.

"You weren't going to hobble on one foot through the sand, were you?"

"Well, if I had to."

He laughed. "Anna, it's hard enough to run in the sand. This is much easier."

"For me, but not for you."

"Trust me, I can handle this," he said. "We're almost there."

"Thank you," was all she could manage as she was hanging upside down with a direct view of his blue-jeaned butt. The ride didn't last long enough for her taste before he gently lowered her back to the ground next to his truck. Her head was not only flushed from her inverted position but also from her excellent view.

His truck beeped as he pushed the button on his key fob, and the doors unlocked. He opened the passenger door for her and lifted her up. "Relax, I'll pull out the bag for you." He opened the back door of his truck. "Found it!"

"Open it up and look for a bottle with distilled water, so I can irrigate the wound."

He rummaged through the medical supplies and found a small bottle. He held it up for her to see. "Is it this one?"

She stretched her neck to see what he had in his hand. "That's it. Just pass it to me. There should also be a plastic irrigation bottle with a nozzle. Do you see it?"

"I think this is it." He handed the empty bottle to her.

She unscrewed the tops of both bottles and filled the irrigation bottle halfway. "While I'm doing this, can you find some gauze pads?" She pulled up her injured foot. It was a mess. Blood and sand had clumped to a gooey-cakey crust on her toe. She squirted a stream of water around it and then onto the wound itself to flush out all the sand and debris. Once it was clean, she assessed the damage. The cut was still bleeding, and the wound was a quarter cm deep, but there wasn't a whole lot she could do right now.

Jason took a peek, then winced.

"Do you have the gauze pads?"

He handed her the sterile packs.

She ripped one open and pressed the gauze onto her wound. Hopefully, it would stop the bleeding soon. While she put pressure against her toe, she gave Jason a reassuring smile. His face sported a greenish-pale hue. "Are you okay?" She had forgotten he didn't do so well with blood.

He nodded.

"I should have some anti-bacterial ointment and wound closure strips in the bag, too." Maybe giving him something to do would keep his mind off her toe.

Jason looked confused.

"You know, those small, skinny Band-Aids?" she added.

Jason nodded, then got busy digging through the bag again. The distraction would do him good.

She checked the wound again, and the bleeding had stopped for the most part. She added a dab of ointment, stuck a wound closure strip over the gash to keep it closed, and covered it with a Band-Aid. "Now, hand me some medical tape, a glove, and the scissors," she instructed. She cut the thumb of the nitrile glove, pulled it over her toe, and taped it down with medical tape. "The glove should keep the sand out," she said.

Jason helped her out of the truck. He held her just a few seconds longer than necessary, then handed her the left flip-flop. "Do you want to put this on?"

"I should." She took it from him and slipped it over her foot. She cleaned up the mess she'd created and put her supplies back into her bag.

As he closed the truck's doors, a large raindrop landed on her head. Hadn't he said it wouldn't rain for another hour or two? She looked up. "I hope that was a raindrop. You don't see any seagulls flying around, do you?"

With a laugh, he shook his head and turned to her. "It's good to have you back as a friend, Weaver. That's what we are, right? Friends?"

Jason knew he'd said something wrong when her laughter faded as soon as he spoke those last words. Guilt gnawed at his conscience as he helped Anna walk to the door of her hotel room in silence. It was best to call it a night for many reasons. For one, they had an early and dangerous day ahead of them. And two, the way she cuddled up to him at the beach reminded him of how they used to spend hours sitting at their secret spot down at the creek on the edge of town, letting their feet dangle in the cool water until the mosquitos came out at dusk. Many times they had lost track of time and both had gotten in trouble for coming home late. Things were different then. They were dating and didn't have a care in the world. Since he'd asked her on this trip, he'd had to constantly remind himself that they were here as friends. Life was complicated now for both of them, and that was the promise he had made to her, as much as he had enjoyed spending time with her.

"Good night, Anna," he said when they arrived at her door. "Get some rest, okay?"

Anna looked down. "Good night, Jason," she said, her voice breaking as she inserted her key card into the lock.

"I'll be next door if you need something, okay?"

She nodded and looked at him one more time before shutting the heavy door on him.

Jason stood there. He was a jerk. A little more tact to reel their emotions back in would've done the job of reminding her of their intention for this trip. They were here to cover a hurricane, not to relive old memories, at least not the way they were heading. Truth was, as happy and nostalgic as he felt today, his love still belonged to Caroline. He had made a vow on their wedding day to love and cherish her till death would part them. Even though she'd been gone for two years now, he didn't have the heart to let go.

Jason raked his hands through his hair. But Anna... They had such a good time today that he almost dreaded that he was on this trip for work. Spending time with her at the beach felt so familiar, as if time skipped two decades of his life and fast forwarded to today. Her laughter was contagious, and she still had the same quirky sense of humor she did when they were teens. He had loved her then, and the longer they'd spent time together as adults, it all came back to him. The dancing sparkle in her eyes still mesmerized him, and all he wanted was to kiss her—really kiss her, not a peck on the forehead—but he couldn't allow himself to go there. It felt like cheating, something he had never even entertained the thought of.

He realized that he still stood in front of her door. Anna's sad eyes and determination not to cry in front of him only a few moments ago made him feel lower than pond scum. He'd disappointed her. The sob that penetrated through the door twisted and pulled his gut. What had he done to her...again?

Jason had to walk away. With his head hanging low and his legs dragging as if they were full of lead, he turned around and walked the few steps to his door. At first his card wouldn't work, and he cussed at it for good measure until he realized he was inserting it the wrong way.

The room was an empty shell without Anna's cheerful company. It was too quiet. As if on cue, the AC unit turned on, filling the room with the loud, clattering hum of the fan. He wasn't sure why he had it running in the first place. All it seemed to do was blow around the hot, humid air.

To distract himself from the guilt of upsetting Anna and questioning his loyalty to Caroline, Jason sat down on his bed and opened his laptop. His inbox was overflowing, but only three messages needed immediate attention. Once he answered them, he tracked the radar one more time and checked on the latest Hurricane

Hunter data, but nothing worked to keep Anna out of his head. He needed to get some sleep. It was already close to midnight, and he had to be alert for tomorrow's stormy conditions and broadcasts. It would be a busy day.

Hot and sticky from the humidity, Jason took off his shirt and noticed two small bloodstains on his jeans. "No!" He had to get those stains out so they wouldn't set on his favorite pair. He dreaded the task, but he had to do it. Jason ran some cool water over the bloody spots and rubbed hotel soap on the stains. The scrubbing discolored the white soap to a reddish brown. He almost gagged when his hands touched the rust-colored foam.

He scrubbed and rinsed the lower leg for about ten minutes until most of the blood washed out. A liberal amount of stain remover and his washing machine should take care of the rest. After he rinsed the bar of soap, he washed his hands, and hung his pants over a chair in front of the air conditioning unit. He hoped that the airflow would dry his pant leg by morning. Not that it mattered when he'd broadcast in pouring, horizontal rain.

He hopped in the shower to rinse the sweat and sea salt off his skin. The lukewarm water was refreshing on his body until he remembered the pain on Anna's face when they ended the evening. Suddenly, the water burned as if acid was pouring down his body. Disgusted with himself, he stepped out of the shower, dried off, and put on boxers. He made a mental note to make amends with Anna in the morning. He had to.

Jason turned on the sink faucet and squirted some toothpaste onto his electric toothbrush. Anna's sad face faded in his mind, but a moment later, it morphed into Caroline's. She was smiling at him. Wasn't he suffering enough already? Was this one of those moments when God wanted to tell you something, he wondered, or was it some sick joke his mind was playing on him? "Okay, I admit I messed up," he said, looking around, not sure what to focus on.

Why did he feel as if someone was watching him? It wasn't a creepy presence but rather a familiar one. Jason wiped a few lines of fog off the mirror, but all he saw was his reflection, toothpaste frothing out of his mouth. Had someone entered his room? He turned and checked the front door for anything unusual, then checked the closet and the balcony. Nothing. He was alone.

Jason stepped back into the steamy bathroom. This strange sensation followed him. It reminded him of when his wife would sneak up from behind him as they were getting ready for work in the mornings. He sensed her standing right beside him, as he had so many times when she was alive. But that was impossible. Was he losing his mind?

The guilt returned. He took the toothbrush out of his mouth and sat it on the edge of the sink. "Caroline? Is that you?" Nobody answered. What did he expect? "Is this some kind of cruel joke? Because if it is, it isn't working," he said. Yet he could still feel the presence, as if the air was heavier around him—not a negative heavy, but a sense of unconditional love. Still, the guilt about the feelings he had for

Anna gnawed at his soul. "I'm sorry, baby," he said. "I don't know what's happening to me. Anna was a good friend of mine. Well, we dated in high school, and she's moved back to town. I'm sorry, I got carried away. I..."

Caroline's smiling face appeared in his mind again, followed by a sense of calmness.

"Caroline, I will keep my promise! I will always be yours."

Sadness filled her beautiful face. She pointed toward Anna's room, laid her hands over her heart, and smiled again, as if to say it's okay. And that was it. Just as fast as she had appeared in his mind, she was gone. The bathroom returned to its ordinary state again, yet the calmness inside prevailed.

Jason blinked and saw his toothpaste dripping onto his arm. He rinsed out his mouth and sat on his bed. He didn't know how to explain what he had just experienced. Strangely enough, he was at peace. He understood what she was trying to tell him. She was releasing him.

Jason folded the covers of his bed back and sat on the edge. On one hand, he had to get some sleep. On the other hand, he needed to make things right with Anna. He owed it to her. The evening had been too short, and he had so much he wanted to tell her. He wanted to laugh with her and be serious when needed, just the way they did twenty years ago. God, how he had missed her, and now she was crying next door.

The thought of her upset broke his heart. He needed to see her, apologize to her, and hold her in his arms all night. Now that he knew Caroline wanted him to love again, she didn't have to tell him twice. What if it was too late? Was the damage already done? He couldn't blame Anna if she didn't want to see his sorry face ever again after how the evening had ended.

Jason didn't do well with what-ifs. Most important of all, he couldn't live with anyone suffering because of him. Life was too short, and as he found out two years ago, tomorrow may never come, especially with a strong Category 2 hurricane staring them in the face.

That was it! He stuck his head out of the balcony door. Good, it had stopped raining, at least for now. He put on a pair of shorts and a T-shirt, grabbed two bottles of water, and headed out the door.

As Jason stood in front of her room, he had doubts. What if she was already asleep? He should have texted her first. He craned his neck, saw a sliver of light shine through the small hole in the door, and let out a deep breath. Jason lifted his hand to knock but paused. What if she didn't want to talk to him? Well, there was only one way to find out.

He knocked at her door. His heart was beating double-time in anticipation.

"Who is it?"

"It's me, Jason," he said and dangled the two bottles of water in front of her peep hole.

"Hang on," she said, her voice muffled. Anna opened the door, but only a crack until the chain snapped tight. Her tear-streaked face brightened.

"Uh, you need to unlatch the lock."

His heart skipped a few beats as he waited for her to open the door for him.

"Yes?"

"I couldn't sleep. Care to join me on the balcony to enjoy the show?" He held up the two bottles of water again and pointed at the glass door at the other end of her room, his heart still working in overdrive.

"Okay."

"May I come in?" he asked.

She nodded, ran the back of her hand over her eyes, and opened the door wide for him.

He frowned when he saw her limping, but she didn't let on if she was in pain. On the balcony, he arranged the two chairs for them so they sat side by side with a perfect view of the dark and roaring sea. He led her to the closest chair and helped her sit down. "Before you say anything, I just wanted to tell you I'm an idiot."

She gave him a tentative nod.

"Look, Anna, this is all new territory for me. When I first saw you again at the park, I felt like we'd never been apart." He held her hand. "I know I promised you we'd go on this chase as friends, but I..."

"I understand," she said. "That was the deal, and I overreacted. I'm not sure what I was expecting..."

Now it was his turn to be perplexed. "No, you didn't overreact. I was a jerk. Truth is, that little kiss on the beach earlier today made my head spin. I always keep my promises, but the minute we were alone watching the waves, something happened to me."

"Same here," she said. "I had firm intentions not to get involved with anyone, not for a long time."

A flash of lightning lit up the sky out at sea. "You know," Jason continued. "I should be in bed resting up, but I had such a good time with you today…"

Anna held up her foot as if to contemplate if she considered losing a toe a good time.

That's why he loved her. "Okay, besides the mishaps and me acting like an insensitive dork, I really enjoyed spending time with you tonight. And I'm not sure how to say this," he stammered, "but I didn't want the evening to end, if that makes sense. I'm sorry. This is a little awkward. It's been a long time since I have talked to a woman I like a lot."

She buried her face in her hands, then raised her head until she met his gaze. "Uh, I was hoping you'd come knocking at my door." Her face flushed even more. "I kinda feel the same way but wasn't sure if, you know..."

"Well," he said. "I'd say, let's just be us. It's not like we haven't known each other for over thirty years."

She laughed. "Gosh, Jason, you make me feel old."

"Anna, you don't look a day under sixty," he said, which earned him a punch in the arm. "No, seriously, you really don't look your age. You so remind me of who you were when we were our kids' age."

"I'm still the same me, Jason."

That she was, and she could still muddle his senses with her beautiful eyes.

She swatted at a mosquito on her leg and knocked her water bottle off the arm of her chair. It landed right between them. Jason bent down to catch it before it rolled away, but they both had the same idea, and their heads collided midway.

"Ouch," she said rubbing the top of her forehead.

Their eyes met. There was no going back now. "Your water," he said, holding up her bottle without breaking eye contact. Lightning flashed and another band of rain hit. "We should go inside," he whispered.

Chapter 10

Anna felt like she'd been in a time machine and was back in high school again, except this time, Jason was taller and more muscular.

She knew Jason was different from Luke. He didn't show any signs of aggression. He was still the same adorable, dorky guy he was back then. Anna knew he would always treat her right. Jason didn't have a mean bone in his body and always treated everyone with respect. It was his nature. She had no reason to fear him lashing out in anger at her like Luke did. Granted, it'd only been a short while since they'd met again, but spending time with him now felt like they'd never been apart.

Her TV was still running on the Weather Channel. She hobbled closer to check the radar. The first hefty band of rain had passed over them with more intense bands to follow later. The now well-defined eye of the hurricane was hovering about eighty miles off the coastline.

"Hey," Jason said, pointing at the TV as he carried in their water bottles. "This is not my station! Are you fraternizing with the competition?"

She shrugged her shoulders as if she didn't care. "Are you suggesting I should consider myself lucky that I have my personal chief meteorologist seeing me through this hurricane?"

"That's a start."

She nodded at the rotating green and orange blob on the screen. "The only reason I have the TV on the Weather Channel is to look at the radar..."

"I could have told you it would rain," he said in a mock I-told-you-so voice. "I'm also predicting that it will be very stormy tomorrow morning. The Weather Channel can't tell you more than I can."

"Oh yeah?"

"Yeah."

She smiled, then added, "Tim Summerville is in town, too."

"Ah, the competition's big-shot star meteorologist. It doesn't surprise me he's covering the storm. Wherever disaster's brewing, he's there," he said with a smirk.

"You don't seem too like him much," she said.

"We used to be roommates in college. He chose to follow the money and worked his way up to broadcast nationally, which also didn't surprise me. He's always been arrogant and condescending. As his income grew, so did his ego."

"Oh. Could've fooled me."

"He hides it well on camera." His facial expression softened. "Why, do you have a little crush on him?" he teased her.

"Maybe," she answered, batting her eyes at him.

"Well, but I'm here...right now...with you."

"Yeah?"

Jason raked his fingers through his hair. "Oh, hell," he said. "Wait right here." He closed her balcony door.

Her heart was beating harder by the second as he slowly came closer. One corner of his mouth pulled up into an impish smile. Oh, my! He was definitely up to no good.

The heat in the room became unbearable. She wasn't sure if it was the air temperature or his presence that made her knees buckle. She fanned herself with one hand. *Come on, AC, kick harder,* she thought. She was already standing under the downdraft of the ceiling fan, but it didn't seem to make a difference. Would he kiss her again?

He stood in front of her now.

She wasn't sure if her heart could handle any more suspense. Her lips tingled in anticipation of what she hoped was another kiss.

He inched closer. His hair was still damp, and random rain drops still lingered on his face and shirt. He raised his hands to cradle her face.

The touch alone made her body tingle. How was she going to survive this? If he kept going, she may not even live to see the hurricane tomorrow.

His lips came closer to hers. Three... two...one...inches.

She closed her eyes, holding her breath, waiting for his lips to meet hers. It seemed like an eternity. She noticed a hint of mint toothpaste as he exhaled. He was close. Any second now.

As soon as their lips touched, she was lost in the familiar sensation of his kiss. At first, he was tentative and gentle. That alone drove her insane.

He took a breath, and his stubble grazed her cheek. "I missed you," he whispered in her ear, then tightened his embrace to pull her closer.

She had no idea how she got there, but somehow she found herself on the upturned bed with Jason caressing her face and back as he gently kissed her. A clap of window-rattling thunder made her jump out of her skin, then the lights flickered off. She could hear the wind howling and the rain drumming on the window. The hurricane had nothing on the emotions Jason stirred up in her. She hadn't been this happy in decades.

* * *

It was still dark when Anna woke to the rattling of her hotel room window. She checked her watch. "Ugh, only four in the morning," she mumbled. Jason was already up and putting on his shorts in the dark. The only light she saw was the bright glow of his cell phone bouncing off the walls.

He walked over to her side of the bed and bent down. "Oh, Anna, I want to cuddle more, but duty calls," he said and kissed her one more time. "I'll either be in my room or down by the storm tracker vehicle with Brandon," he said, then walked toward the door of her room.

She nodded, rubbing the sleep out of her eyes. "Hmmm…"

A scraping sound followed by a few thuds stopped him in his tracks. Jason turned toward the sound.

Anna's heart skipped a beat, and she clutched her hand to her chest. "What was that?"

Jason crossed the room and looked out the balcony door to investigate.

"Can you see?" she asked.

The scraping sound continued, followed by another bang.

Jason turned and smiled at her, his cell phone light casting a shadow behind him on the wall. "It's the chairs. The wind has picked up considerably."

 "Let me get these plastic chairs inside before they blow away, or break something," he said. He opened her balcony door. In an instant, a gust of wind ripped the door out of his hand and slammed it against the wall. A bolt of lightning illuminated the room, and rain and debris blew in.

"Aaaah, forget about the chairs and close the door!" she yelled in panic. If she hadn't been awake before, she was now.

"Sorry about that," he said, fighting to shut the door behind him. "Get more rest, sweetheart. It'll be a busy day." He kissed her one more time, then exited her room. "I'll come and get you before the broadcast, okay?"

The latch clicked, and it was dark again. *Thank goodness for hotel blackout curtains*, she thought. Another round of sleep would have been perfect—if it wasn't for all the commotion outside of her room. Speaking of sleep, she almost didn't get any last night. They had kissed, snuggled, and reminisced about their teenage years until she fell asleep in his arms. Fast forward to now, and it was tempting to stay in bed...and miss the hurricane? No way!

A surge of excitement coursed through her body. It was already starting. Just because she only got a few hours of sleep didn't mean she wasn't ready for Gerard. Working as a paramedic had its perks. She had learned to nap between runs and be clearheaded and ready when the next call came in. This morning wasn't an exception.

Anna sat up in her bed and checked her cell phone. A long list of weather warnings filled her lock screen. Anna threw her head back and laughed. "Yes!" She kicked the sheet off her feet and rolled out of bed. With the help of her phone, she searched the nightstand for the flashlight she had brought in the likely case they would lose power. The space by the lamp was empty. Had Jason used it? She searched her room but had no luck finding it. Maybe he took it with him. No, he wouldn't leave her in the dark like that. She had to find it so she could conserve her phone battery to stay in touch with her mom and daughter.

"No, no, no!" she muttered, turning over pillows, checking the covers, and searching the floor. Nothing. She grunted as she pushed herself to her feet. Push-ups and knee-bends were never her thing, forget this early in the morning.

Anna plopped onto the bed again. It couldn't have vanished. She shone her light back onto the nightstand and discovered a gap between the wall and the furniture. Had the wind knocked it over when Jason opened the balcony door? Hopeful, she stretched to look behind the furniture and held her phone over the gap. There it was, hanging halfway down the wall where it had gotten stuck in a spot where the gap narrowed. With some creative contortions, she reached it with her fingertips and pulled it out of its hiding place. Anna pushed the rubber flashlight button, and the room lit up enough for her to see without stumbling over furniture. She turned off her phone's flashlight to conserve power and stood the flashlight upright on her nightstand.

It had been hot and sticky in the room since they'd lost power last night. She limped over to the window and pushed the curtain aside. Her toe still throbbed, but not as bad as it did last night. She still had plenty of ibuprofen in her purse to last her through the weekend. Anna made a mental note to take a dose with some food before she joined Jason and Brandon and put a few pills in a plastic baggy to carry with her.

Looking out on the nighttime beach, she could only see within the reach of the flood lights of the news crews prepping for their first broadcasts. Watching reporters battling the wind and rain reminded her of hurricane reports gone wrong again. A smile crossed her face. How many times had she, Jason, and Sean made fun of them on TV during stormy weather? Watching them live was just as entertaining.

Seeing the crews struggle, she almost gave in to the temptation to stay in her room and wait for the rainband to pass. But that would mean she'd also miss out on the hurricane experience. Wasn't that the reason she traveled to Tybee Island in the first place, to get her stormy weather fix? Well, one of the reasons. Jason was the other.

The flashes of lightning slowed, so she opted to risk taking a quick, cold shower to cool off. She might not have a chance later on. They'd be lucky if the hotel even survived Gerard. She shook her head. Of course it would. Jason wouldn't put them in danger.

As the initial shock of the cold water eased, she thought back to last night. It had been bliss lying in his arms, and for a moment, she'd been seventeen again. His kisses and sweet words had been so tender, she hadn't wanted the night to end. A smile escaped her.

He really still loves me, she thought as she shampooed her hair. She massaged the soap into her scalp, then dropped her hands altogether and let the water do the rinsing.

Then a thought struck her. Were they moving too fast? She froze. They had shared such a tender moment last night, but this was reality. Even though they were only hugging and kissing and falling asleep in each other's arms, it was more than what "friends" would do. They had moved too fast, way too fast! The agreement was that they were at Tybee as friends, nothing else. She just went through a divorce. Heading from one relationship into another wasn't a good idea. What had happened to turn her entire world upside down since her return to Magnolia Hill? Anna knew exactly what, and better yet...who. Jason.

But what if she was overreacting? She had known him for years. One could say they grew up together. What was she going to do? Love had a way of messing with her usually good judgment. She turned off the shower, squeezed the water out of her hair, and stepped onto the towel on the bathroom floor. For a moment, she stood dripping. Anna cupped her face in her hands and let out an agonized growl followed by a stomp—with her bad foot. "Aaaah!" she called out as pain shot from her toe up her lower leg. Why was her life so complicated?

After she brushed her teeth, Anna checked her injured toe and re-wrapped it with the extra supplies she had brought in from the night before. It didn't throb as much anymore, but it was still sore when she tried to walk on it. If only the warning sirens in her head would also subside.

There was no point in doing anything with her hair, so she just put it in a ponytail and pulled it through the loop of her ball cap. She had to tighten the fit, because chances were that the hurricane would blow it right off her head if she wasn't careful.

She moved the curtain aside and peeked out of the window. It was daybreak—not that it would be a bright day, but she now had enough light to turn off her flashlight.

Half-starved, she rummaged through her cooler for some bottled water and something edible for breakfast before she joined Jason and Brandon. She made a quick sandwich, and once it was gone, she attempted to peel one of the hard-boiled eggs her mom had packed for them yesterday morning. Someone must have super-glued the shell to the egg. Chunks of the egg-white chipped off with each piece of shell, leaving her with a mangled half-peeled mass of protein.

Small debris kept hitting her window, distracting Anna, who lost patience with her breakfast. Losing interest in food was unusual for her, but right then, she'd rather be out in the elements experiencing a hurricane with Jason. Besides, she wanted an update about the current strength of the hurricane and if the eye would still travel over them.

Anna packed away the unfinished food for later, put on her windbreaker, and headed down to the lobby. The wind was fierce and whistling through the cracks of the rattling glass sliding door of the main entrance. She lifted the hood over her ball cap and tightened the strings. She tucked her room key into her jeans pocket. "Here goes nothing!"

As soon as she stepped out into the elements, a strong wind gust almost knocked her down to the ground. She had expected it to be windy, but she wasn't ready for this. What was worse, Gerard hadn't even made landfall yet.

Rain pricked her face and legs like needles.

"Ouch!" she cried out. Debris was flying past her, missing her by inches. She had to get out of this mess.

The storm tracker vehicle should still be in the parking lot right around the corner to protect it best from the hurricane-force winds. She made her way along the building, trying to hold on to solid objects, such as beams and rails, in case a gust caught her. The last thing she wanted was the wind picking her up and becoming the subject of a viral hurricane video.

Halfway there, she realized she could have gone out the side door. Too late now. Her toe throbbed, but it was the last thing she was worried about now.

As she made it around the corner, she saw Bessie parked close to the building. Relieved, she walked toward the storm tracker vehicle. Now that she was in the building's shadow, the wind and rain decreased in an instant. She spotted the hotel's side door and shook her head. It figured.

"Hey Anna," Brandon said, preparing his camera for the extreme weather. "Isn't that somethin'?" he asked, nodding out to sea.

Anna nodded. "It sure is. I almost got blown away!"

He laughed. "Why didn't you use the side door?"

She rolled her eyes. "I know. I learned the hard way."

Brandon pointed to Bessie's open back doors. "Jason's in the van."

She walked toward the back end of the storm tracker vehicle. When she heard his voice, she forgot all about the pain and trouble she'd gone through to join them.

Jason was on his cell phone. His face brightened when he saw her, and he waved. "Yes," he said, focusing on his call. "So, to confirm, Hurricane Hunters report a wind speed of one hundred and eight miles per hour sustained winds near the eye, and we are expecting the storm to make landfall at eight forty on Tybee?" He paused. "Yes, we will hunker down when it gets bad." He hung up the phone and turned his attention to the radar in front of him. "Look, Anna," he said. "We are almost right between rainbands."

"You can't tell by the wind," she said.

"It'll come and go, but be ready for it to get much stronger as the eyewall nears. We will have to take shelter soon, but Brandon and I will knock out a few mini broadcasts before then."

It was beyond her comprehension how much stronger this storm could get. Anna was amazed by the brute force of it so far, and a little terrified. Today marked her first time in the path of a hurricane at ground zero. She began having doubts about joining them. Her instincts told her to take cover now. There was chasing weather for adventure, and there was sheer craziness. If those weren't even the strongest winds yet, they'd be in for a helluva ride. It was too late to turn and run. Gerard had already made his presence known.

She looked out the window. "You guys are nuts," she said.

Both men grinned at her. "And you

aren't?" Jason asked. "Let's shoot a bit of footage while we can."

Anna shook her head. "Go for it! I hope you have good insurance."

Jason winked at her. "Come on, Anna. Don't be a chicken. Are you coming?"

Chapter 11

Jason helped Anna out of the van. She looked terrified but thrilled, as if on a roller-coaster about to topple over the edge. "I'm glad Colorado didn't make you too soft."

"Trust me, it didn't!"

They set up at the end of the parking lot where they had a good vantage point of tree branches whipping in the hurricane-strength winds. They now were even more exposed to anything that wasn't bolted down. Small debris flew through the air, nearly missing them, but that didn't stop the courageous weather team.

Jason turned to check on Anna, who struggled to keep her eyes open with the wind and rain pelting her face. Maybe he had asked too much of her. "Anna, it'd make me feel a lot better if you stood closer to the building and out of the wind," he told her. God forbid she get hit by something. He could never forgive himself should something happen to her. Maggie would kill him if she got hurt.

To his relief, she nodded and backed up toward the hotel and out of the wind, where she would be safer. At least she was out of the path of the flying debris.

While Brandon set up the camera, Jason ran through his report in his mind. The eye of Gerard was only an hour away from making landfall as a strong Category 2 hurricane. Winds would get twice as intense as they already were.

He waved at Anna to let her know he hadn't forgotten about her. How could he ever? Last night was magical. He remembered her sweet kisses on his lips. When she fell asleep in his arms, he had chastised himself for being such a knucklehead when he broke up with her after prom. Now was his chance to make up for his mistakes. Jason counted his lucky stars for having a second chance with Anna. He couldn't blow it this time! He wouldn't.

Jason's weather report focused on the winds and rain as they came closer to the eye's arrival. Covering bending trees, almost strained to their snapping point, and wobbling street signs was the best way to demonstrate the force of this monster storm. "We will be right here covering landfall, so stay tuned," Jason said.

Before he had a chance to turn the report over to the studio, his vision went black. "What the...?" he stopped mid-sentence as he struggled to inhale. What just happened? He couldn't tell if he was still standing and the wind was blowing at him or if he had fallen and gravity was pushing down on him. Disoriented, he groped at his face with his free hand so he could breathe again and felt something other than his wet skin. He pulled the culprit away from his face and gasped. In his hand, he held a giant brown lawn bag that now clung to his torso and leg. He peeled it away from his body and let the wind blow it way. "Folks, as you can see, it's dangerous out here, so please take shelter if you're close to this storm. Flying debris can be lethal."

"Well, thank you, Jason, for braving the elements today," the news anchor said. He could tell that she was suppressing a laugh, too, but to her credit, she kept her professional appearance. "Be safe out there and stay tuned for more updates on Hurricane Gerard."

"Wahaha!" Brandon laughed, holding his midsection with one hand as he lowered his camera. "That was classic! Beware of your lawn bags and store them in a closed container. They can become dangerous projectiles in a hurricane."

Jason glared at him for good measure, then laughed too. "Yeah, that was one for the books." They grabbed the gear and moved closer to the building for safety.

Anna came over and joined them. She looked at him funny, plucked at his hair, and pulled something out. She held a gooey, purplish-green substance between her thumb and index finger. "Is this seaweed?"

Jason rolled his eyes. This broadcast had been a disaster. "You let me go on the air like this?"

Both nodded. "It added to the authenticity of your report, Jason," Anna said.

"You know, one of the major hazards of hurricanes is flying seaweed. Warn the people of what's heading their way!" Brandon chuckled as he wiped his camera lens. "Let's eat something and prep for the next broadcast. Anna, will you join us for a quick bite?" Brandon winked at her.

She rolled her eyes. "As opposed to leaving me here by myself to meet Gerard?" she asked. "Yeah, I'll come with you."

"I still have some sandwiches in my cooler in my room," Jason suggested. "We'll have to be quick, though. We only have a small window to film anything before we have to seek shelter. Technically, we already should be huddling in a safe place by now."

"So why are we still standing here?" she asked. "Let's eat!"

They entered the hotel through the side door and took the stairs up. The wind whistled through cracks in the building. Although there was no wind inside his room, the fortified windows rattled in their frames.

"Best ever sandwiches," Anna said with a full mouth. "Thank you!"

He couldn't pin it down, but Anna seemed to be more distant today. Last night, they were so close, and this morning, she had distanced herself and was now sitting opposite from him. Maybe it was just his imagination. Did she have regrets about last night? He hoped not. Since the moment he had run into her, his life hadn't been the same. She was the light that had entered his darkness. If it wasn't for Brandon sitting right between them, he would ask her about it. Brooding over stuff was never his thing. He'd rather know what prompted this subtle shift in her behavior than make up scenarios in his head that served no one.

Breakfast was over in a record ten minutes. They headed to Bessie, who still stood in the building's shadow, protected from most of the storm's effects, but it wasn't perfect. The wind was blowing stronger than before they took their break, and they struggled to get to the vehicle.

Jason could hear Anna talking to Maggie on her phone in the

background as he got the latest numbers on Gerard. "The girls are fine," she called out to him. "They are still sleeping."

Jason wanted to talk to Sarah one more time, but he didn't want to wake the girls up after staying up late. He knew they would be okay with Maggie. "Can I talk to your mom really quick?"

"Of course," Anna said and handed him her phone.

"Hi, Maggie," he said. "Look, I only have a few minutes to talk."

"I know, Jason," she said. "The girls and Grady are doing fine, and we're safe."

"Stay on the lower levels of the house until the worst is over, and as always, thank you so much for letting her stay with you. I will see you when we get back, okay?"

"That's fine. We'll keep watching on TV."

"Bye, Maggie," he said and handed the phone back to Anna.

Then his own phone rang. He answered the call from the TV station. "Yes, we're almost ready for the next broadcast. We'll stage it in the stairwell of one of the neighboring hotels so we can see out to the beach."

"Don't do anything stupid," the station manager warned him.

"You know I won't."

"Well, I saw your trash bag incident. I just need to make sure you're safe. We can't afford the liability, and," she admitted, "we need you around here."

"I'll be careful," he said, just to appease her.

Once he got all his facts, he turned his attention to Anna. "What have the kids been up to?"

"Mom said they worked on making bracelets all night to sell at the store." She smiled, which almost made his heart burst. Oh, how he had missed her.

"They're sleeping in the guest room downstairs because of the storm, and Grady got the couch."

"How's the weather in Magnolia Hill?" he asked.

She looked at him as if he had horns growing out of his head. "Uh, you're the weatherman."

"Sometimes what we see on radar or on our equipment doesn't tell the entire story. That's why we still have weather watchers on the ground."

"Well, Mom said it wasn't too bad. They had a lot of rain and some thunderstorms overnight, but the wind isn't too strong at the moment. The usual roads are flooding. Someone said that the county road heading west is getting bad."

He had expected that, especially after last night's report of Gerard slowing down. The good news was, once the eye made landfall, the storm should weaken and make a sharp turn to the north. He knew they would be safe, if all went well.

"All right, Brandon," Jason said. "Are you ready?"

His friend nodded.

"And you, Anna?"

"Ready," she answered.

They exited the van and went up the outer stairs of the neighboring hotel to get a better view of the swirling clouds and the angry ocean. "We will do a short broadcast right here where we're more protected, and then head back downstairs and hunker down in the hallway by the lobby to wait for the eye," he shouted over the howling wind.

He watched Anna give up on her Broncos ball cap and secure her ponytail in a bun after her hair kept whipping her face. She had no idea how much he adored her just now.

"I think this is a great spot," Brandon said and motioned out to the sea. *Leave it to Brandon to ruin the perfect moment,* he thought.

Besides the storm surge, the tide was coming in, flooding most of the beach by now. From his vantage point, he could see lawn chairs on the bottom of the neighboring hotel pool. That was one way of securing them from the wind. He could also see the damage Gerard had already caused on roofs, signs, and billboards, and the worst hadn't even arrived yet.

The broadcast only lasted a few minutes, and then the trio retreated to the relative safety of the first floor hallway of their hotel to wait for the eye. The wind was howling and they could hear thumps and crashes when debris impacted the building or broke a window.

Anna sat next to him. He could tell she was scared but too tough to show it. He searched for her hand, and when he found it, laced his fingers through hers. She nearly crushed his bones.

Chapter 12

Anna had not expected the intensity of the storm to ramp up so fast. She had never experienced the sounds and strength of a Category 2 hurricane before in person. By the time those storms reached Magnolia Hill, most were downgraded to tropical storms, and the only risk was local flooding and maybe some wind damage. Not this time! Never had she heard an entire building this sturdy moan and creak like this one. Anna was certain it would give in to the force of these powerful gusts and get blown away any minute now. She was terrified.

"Are you sure we're safe?" she asked Jason.

He wrapped his arm around her shoulders and gave her an assuring squeeze. "I hope so."

"You know, you're not helping," she replied. She had to talk Jason about their relationship at one point, but now was not the time. Instead, she needed him to keep her safe. His arm provided some comfort, even if it was just a distraction from the relentless howl of the wind outside.

Brandon laughed, entirely enjoying this experience. What a nut! Watching him reminded her of Dusty from the '90s movie *Twister*, her favorite disaster movie when she was a teenager. She could feel the adrenaline course through her body. It was a mixture of extreme excitement and deathly fear that made this moment so intense. She wasn't sure how much more of the suspense she could handle.

The sound of glass breaking nearby made her jump.

"We're okay," Jason said and held her tighter. "Only a few more minutes, and we'll punch through the eyewall."

The wall she leaned against moved and vibrated with every gust. She looked down the hallway and realized that the entire building was slightly swaying. "It's gonna go!" she called out and looked for something to hold on to. There was nothing in reach, so she held on to Jason's leg. Maybe she held on a little too tight, judging by the pained expression on his face, but she couldn't let go.

 Suddenly, the noise stopped. It was over. Anna looked around. "Are we dead?" she asked. It was the strangest sensation. The air pressure changed, and everything seemed to settle outside. It was quiet, and her ears were popping.

"This is it. We're in the eye," Brandon said. "Let's head to the beach and get our footage!"

Jason pulled her up from the floor. "Man, Anna, that was some death grip. I didn't know you were that strong."

She blushed. "I'm sorry. I didn't mean to hurt you."

"Darling, I've been through worse." He kept her hand in his as they walked down the hall.

The words just friends kept running through her head. "Hey look!" She withdrew her hand from his and pointed at the lobby door. A lounge chair had crashed through the glass and left a mess of shards on the floor near the entrance.

She wasn't sure why, but Jason used the side of his hiking boot to clear a path for her as they walked through the crunchy glass shards. Even though it wasn't necessary, his thoughtful gesture flattered her. Thank God she'd worn sneakers, even though they made her toe throb like there was no tomorrow. She made a mental note to check on it later.

As she stepped outside, she was struck with awe. The first thing she noticed was the clear blue sky above them surrounded by a gray wall of swirling clouds.

"Wow. We are extremely lucky to see the eye this clear," Jason said.

"Most time of the time, lower level clouds mess up what could be a beautiful shot," Brandon added as he captured the moment on camera.

She always thought it was beautiful to watch scenes of the eye in disaster movies. But seeing the blue eye in an actual hurricane was beautiful beyond words. The air was calm, almost eerie, compared to the winds raging only minutes ago. Her eyes scanned the buildings and scenery around her. That's when she saw the destruction in front of her. Sturdy trees lay in the middle of the road, pieces of buildings were missing or caved in, and trash littered the parking lot.

"Whoa!" Brandon said, as he looked around. "Freakin' awesome!"

Anna had to admit, from a coolness factor, this was a ten. From the point of view of people affected by this storm, it was catastrophic. Gerard would impact everyone on this island in one way or another.

They walked toward the storm tracker vehicle.

"Hey! Check this out!" Brandon called out and pointed at Bessie. "This is awesome."

A splintered 2x4 stuck halfway through the windshield on the passenger side.

"Impressive, but our station manager won't be as happy as you are about this," Jason said as he assessed the damage. "We'll see if Bessie survives round two. Not much we can do about the windshield now. Hang in there, Bessie," he said patting the van for good measure. "Brandon, let's set up at the beach while we're in the eye. We don't have much time before the wind kicks up again."

His camera man nodded.

"Are you okay, Anna?" Jason asked.

"I'm fine," she said.

As they headed to the beach, Jason made a call to the station to notify them they were ready to broadcast in a few minutes.

"We're glad you haven't been blown away yet," the producer said over the speaker on Jason's cell.

While they were talking shop, Anna also took the opportunity to call Maggie. She was worried about her and Ashleigh after what she'd just gone through. "Mom, I just wanted to let you know we're fine. We're in the eye right now."

"Thank God!" she replied. "I was so worried about you."

"Are you guys okay?" Anna asked.

"We're fine," Maggie said. "It's gotten windy, but nothing extreme. The girls and Grady are still sleeping, if you believe it." She laughed. "Them kids made a whole basket of bracelets last night," she said, her southern accent more pronounced.

Anna couldn't help but smile. There was a hurricane on their doorstep and they'd slept right through it. "Jason is about to do another broadcast from the beach."

"I kept the TV running all night long. We have a tornado watch, so I'll keep my eyes open. I talked to the kids last night about what our emergency plans are, come worst-case scenario."

She knew she could count on her mom. She'd always been the organized and efficient one in the family. "I love you, Mom!"

"I love you, too, sweetie. Promise me you won't do anything stupid?"

"I promise. I have to go, though. Please give Ash a kiss from me, even if she doesn't like it. Actually, she does, but she doesn't like to show it."

Maggie laughed again. "I know, darling. She's a lot like you, believe it or not. She's definitely not a hugger or kisser."

Anna blushed. She'd done a lot of both last night. Her mom was right, though. She'd been more of a tomboy as a kid, thinking all that huggy-kissy stuff was for the hoity-toity girls, not her. Instead, she'd been more interested in how to get her hands muddy. Jenna hadn't been able to stand it when Anna was a mess. But it had been Anna who'd gotten rid of the spiders and palmetto bugs in the room when they had sleepovers.

"Well, Mom, I'll call you again when this next part of the storm is over. Love ya!" she said and hung up the phone. Her battery was almost dead. She'd have to get a fresh battery pack from her room next time she wanted to make a call.

They arrived at the beach. The scene took her breath away. The ocean covered the beach where they'd stood just last night watching the lightning display, courtesy of Gerard. Looking ahead, she could make out where the eyewall separated the blue calm from the gray, raging storm. The sun shone through the hole in the clouds. "Wow!"

"I think this is a good spot. What do

you think?" Brandon asked, and set up his camera.

Jason surveyed the scene. "Perfect, we have the pier in the shot, so viewers can use it as a reference point for the water level. At the same time, we have a gorgeous shot of the eyewall." He wrapped his arm around her shoulders again and pointed out to the ocean. "Isn't this amazing?"

Anna didn't return his embrace. Just friends. It should have been a magical moment, watching the calm before the storm kicked up again for part two of its destructive power. She wondered how many people got a chance to see this phenomenon in their lifetime. She was one of the few, but somehow it wasn't as glorious as she had hoped. Trying to salvage the moment, she wrapped her arm around his waist, but it felt forced.

Jason looked at her, confused.

"Hey, Jason, are you ready? We only have a small window to cover the eye," Brandon urged.

"Yeah, I'm ready." Jason dropped his arm. "We'll talk later, okay?"

Brandon gave Jason a thumbs up.

"Hello, folks, Chief Meteorologist Jason Morrison here, giving you a live report from Tybee Island. We are in the eye of Hurricane Gerard. As you can tell, we have very little wind, and the sky above us is clear blue. But don't let this serenity fool you. As soon as the eyewall passes through the area, highly destructive winds will resume. The danger from here on out will be hurricane-force winds blowing from the opposite direction. Already weakened structures will get blasted from the opposite side, which could make them unstable or even collapse," he warned the audience. "The good news is that Gerard has weakened to a Category 1 hurricane with sustained wind speed measured at ninety-four miles per hour and gusts at one hundred and one miles per hour. We expect it to downgrade to a tropical storm in about an hour or two. Again, a tropical storm can still produce significant damage. We are also lucky that Gerard has picked up speed and is now moving along. This means flooding will not be a huge factor anymore, except for the folks living close to the coastline and near rivers. As you can see, we have quite a bit of storm surge. Luckily for the residents of Tybee Island, we are at low tide at the moment, but we may have some issues later on as the tide returns. I will keep a close eye on this as Gerard passes over us."

Anna noticed that the sky was darkening again, and the wind had picked up. Her common sense told her to run for cover now.

Jason looked up. "Folks, it looks like we're about to exit the eyewall." He looked at Brandon for confirmation to keep going. "We'll stay here for a few more moments to demonstrate how fast these conditions can change."

Anna shook her head. "Are you nuts?" she mouthed, but she knew she couldn't change his mind.

"Anna, run for cover now!" he urged her. "Pardon me, I just want to make sure that my crew is safe," he continued. "My cameraman and I will continue reporting for a minute and then go for shelter ourselves. Don't do this at home," he warned the audience.

Gerard's backside made his presence known in only a few short moments. "As you can tell, hurricane-force winds have picked up again..." Jason yelled into the wind.

This isn't right, Anna thought. It wasn't safe. She gave them the cut-it-out sign as she saw random beach toys and things flying through the air, but Jason ignored her. All she could do was press herself against the hotel wall and hope for the best and pray the two men wouldn't get hurt.

"All right," Jason said. "It's getting dangerous out here. We'll have to take..."

Anna watched in horror as a large plywood panel tumbled across the beach, aiming right for the pair.

"Watch out!" she yelled.

The rest of the disaster played out in front of her in slow motion. Jason looked to his left, eyes and mouth wide in horror, then Brandon caught on. "Oh, sh—"

She watched them duck, but it was too late. The rogue piece of plywood struck them and knocked them down onto the sand.

Chapter 13

The instant the panel flew away, Anna's paramedic training kicked in. She assessed the scene. Both men were lying on the beach. Brandon stirred and sat up, touching his head to see if he was bleeding, then got up and disconnected his camera from its tripod. He pointed the camera at Jason.

Unbelievable! Was he still filming?

Jason, on the other hand, didn't move. Her heart raced. Please let him be okay! She checked to see if it was safe enough to get to them, then ran through the sand. She first reached Brandon. He had a red spot on his head but was moving around just fine —a little slow for her liking, but at least he was upright and alert.

"Wicked!" he said with a grin pasted on his face.

"Are you okay?"

He nodded and refocused his camera on Jason. "Hey, we're still alive," he said. "Cool!"

"Seriously?" Anna shook her head, then moved over to Jason, who still lay motionless in the sand. "Jason, wake up!" she shouted over the wind while checking if he was breathing and looking for a pulse. She saw his chest rise and fall and picked up a thready pulse. "Thank God," she said, more to herself as she continued to assess his injuries. "Come one, Jason, wake up," she tried again. "You don't want to miss the second half of this hurricane, do you?" He had a nasty gash on the right side of his forehead about half an inch above his eye. It was bleeding profusely, as many facial injuries do. "Wake up, Jason!" she tried again, this time louder and shaking him more forcefully to pull him back to consciousness. He stirred, then opened his eyes.

"Hello, baby!" he said with a weak smile and confusion written all over his face.

"Don't baby me! That was stupid! Stupid, stupid, stupid!" She checked his eyes. Good, both pupils were equal. "Tell me your name," she demanded.

"Chief Meteorologist Jason Morrison, ma'am."

He definitely still had his cheeky sense of humor. "Not funny! What day of the week is it?"

"Saturday."

She nodded. At least he didn't have an altered mental status. "How many fingers am I holding up?"

He focused for a moment. "Three."

"Good. Do you feel nauseous?"

"Somewhat."

"I'm going to go run and get my medic bag from the truck. I'll need the keys."

Jason dug in his pocket and handed her the key fob.

"Brandon, get him off this beach and over to the building," she instructed.

Anna ran back to the hotel, hoping she wouldn't be the next person to get knocked out by airborne debris. She dodged a trashcan lid, a beach umbrella, and a few other flying objects on her way, cursing Jason's name with every one of them that missed her.

Somehow, she made it to the truck alive, grabbed the bag, and slammed the door shut behind her. Her toe throbbed as though it was going to explode inside of her shoe. What had Jason been thinking putting them in danger like that? If it wasn't for her legal duty to help them, she could have just left them there to deal with their own stupidity. It was tempting because she was putting herself in danger, but in reality, she knew she'd do everything in her power to save her now patients.

Anna did the same dance trying to avoid debris on her way back to the lunatic news crew, but this time, her limp was more pronounced. She really had to check on her foot when they were back in the hotel hallway. Anna stomped through the sand and arrived at the pathetic pile of news people.

To his credit, Brandon had dragged Jason to safety, but the camera was still trained on him. "Folks, medical care is very limited in an evacuated area. First responders won't be able to respond until the danger is over, and even then, roads may be impassible. So, don't do what we just did," he said with a sheepish grin.

"You're dang right," Anna scolded them. "You could have been killed. Both of you!"

"If you're still watching, this is Anna Weaver, a paramedic who joined us this weekend to cover this developing story."

Brandon zoomed his camera in on Anna.

She kicked him in the shin. That's all she needed now, to be featured on TV.

"Ouch!" he feigned.

"Hold still!" she fussed at Jason while digging through her medical supplies. She dug out her penlight and checked if his pupils were reactive to light, then irrigated his wound. She cleaned his face with gauze pads as she waited for the bleeding to slow, then applied two wound closure strips to hold the gash together. The wind blew her trash and some of her supplies away, so she grabbed necessary items, shoved them in her pocket, and re-zipped her bag. She applied some ointment and a large Band-Aid to his wound. "You're done reporting this storm," she ordered.

He sighed. "You heard the paramedic. I will now send you back into the capable hands of Meteorologist Mike Evans at the studio."

Brandon lowered his camera and laughed. "That was awesome," he said, "and I got it all on camera."

Anna shook her head. "Not awesome!" she yelled at them. "You two could have been killed out there, and for what, a few moments of fame?"

Jason looked defeated. "I just wanted to show the audience how sudden the weather can change in a hurricane."

"And look at you two! Was it worth it?" she shouted over the wind. She grabbed her bag and limped through the broken glass door into the hotel lobby. "Are you coming, or do you want to take another shot getting killed out there?" She was so furious she couldn't even see straight. She tossed her bag onto the spot they'd sat on earlier, then plopped down herself. Not even acknowledging the two men, she texted her mom to vent. *I know u just saw what happened 2 these idiots. We're ok. Jason & Brandon r lucky 2 b alive. Luck of the stupid. Mom, why did I come out here?*

Her phone dinged a few seconds later. Honey, it's in your blood and soul, the text read. *Remember, you live for this stuff, and so do they. You would have regretted every moment if you hadn't gone. Tell me I'm wrong...*

She loved her mom, not only because she always could see right through her but because she always spoke the truth. Maggie was right about this whole scenario. She wouldn't want to be anywhere else right now. She felt the anger subside.

* * *

Jason's head throbbed, and there was nothing he could do about it. The hurricane was raging again outside, but not quite with the same intensity as just thirty minutes ago. They sat out the worst of the storm in the hotel hallway again. The walls of the building were swaying and groaning once more, but this time, Anna was one hundred percent in medic mode. She kept checking their vital signs, making sure that they didn't have any other symptoms of traumatic brain injuries—at least that was what she had told them.

"You passed out, and you were nauseous, Jason. These are signs of a concussion," she said as she did the penlight thing on him again. "You better tell me if you feel anything new that's not normal."

He grinned, but when she gave him that stern look, as if laser beams would shoot out of her eyes any second, he forced his face to take on a more neutral expression. *Let's just hope she can't read minds,* he thought.

As the winds settled, a familiar face passed them in the hall. "Well, look, if it isn't internet sensation Jason Morrison," Tim Summerville said before giving a less than an honest smile. "I haven't seen you in years."

"Hi, Tim. So we meet again." Jason got to his feet. "What do you mean internet sensation?"

"It's all over social media"—he pointed to Jason's bandage—"the way you got knocked in the head with that plywood. Your video went viral!"

Jason shot a glare at Brandon, who gave an apologetic shrug.

"Hey, I couldn't resist."

Jason rolled his eyes. "Tim, this is my cameraman, Brandon, and my paramedic friend, Anna."

Anna got to her feet, too. She looked starstruck, but he couldn't blame her. The girls always flocked to smooth-talking Tim. Despite Gerard's powerful winds, his hair still looked perfectly groomed. Jason wondered if he used shellac as his favorite weatherproof hair product. No doubt, the board that hit Brandon and him would've just bounced off his helmet head.

Tim flashed a smile, showing off his perfect white teeth. "Anna, it's a pleasure to meet you. Jason is a lucky man to have you around," he said with his well-practiced superstar expression, and Jason could tell how she was melting away. "You've patched him up very well. I should get a medic on my team, too. Knock on wood, nothing's happened to me so far covering dangerous weather."

He wanted to punch Tim, but he thought better of it. He'd be out of town as soon as the weather cleared, anyway.

"Thank you," Anna said. "But I'm just tagging along. I'm not really part of the team."

"Oh? I forget, local stations have small budgets." A smirk crossed Tim's face. "I still can't fathom why you wanted to work for a rural outfit."

His fists tightened. Yes, Savannah was a smaller city, but it was the people, the tight-knit community, that brought him back. "It's what I like," he said through clenched teeth.

"Well, Jason," Tim said, slapping his hand on Jason's shoulder. "It was good to chat and meet your team. I'm glad you made it out of this storm upright."

Jason couldn't say the same about Tim, so he just nodded.

Tim turned to leave but paused a moment. "You know, that was a dumb thing to do," he said and shook his head in disbelief. He threw his hand up in the air in a casual wave. "See you around!"

"What a jerk!" Brandon said.

The sparkle in Anna's eyes was gone. "I think I've changed my mind about Tim Summerville. Has he always been like that?"

"Pretty much."

"Why didn't you warn me?" she asked.

"Would you have believed me?"

"Probably not."

As much as he hated Tim, he was right. Jason had really mucked this one up. Not only had he endangered his team, he'd also put Anna's life at risk by making her go get her medical supplies to save his sorry butt. It was a stupid decision that he now regretted.

They settled back down in the hallway. The mood had dropped to a depressing low. Jason wanted to talk to Anna alone, but there wasn't a private place to do so. Besides, Brandon was too eager to get the scoop on their relationship. Instead, they sat in silence, while Anna kept an eye out for any signs of worsening in their conditions. They would have a chance to talk on their way home. He needed to know what was bothering her. As for himself, he couldn't be any happier. He still loved her, and from the way she snuggled with him last night, maybe she did, too. What had happened since then? Did she have regrets? Had he moved too fast for her? He hung his head in his hands. It drove him insane not knowing what he had done wrong.

Anna bent over and angled her head so she could see his face. "Is your pain getting worse?"

Jason lifted his head and motioned at his heart. "Yes, my heart hurts. I'm in agony!" he said, trying to make light of the situation.

She punched him on his arm. "Yep, still the same Jason…"

After another agonizing hour, the winds let up, and it was safe to go outside. Rain smacked him in the face, and within moments his clothes were drenched again. Debris cluttered the streets and parking lots, and more than once, he had to help Anna with her bad foot over some obstacles.

"Anna," he began, trying to sound as persuasive as possible. "Our viewers depend on our reports. Are you okay with us doing one more quick broadcast?"

"You know, you shouldn't be doing anything right now. You were seriously injured."

"I promise to be short." He flashed her the same grin he knew she couldn't resist.

She sighed. "I'll give you five minutes!"

"Okay, you heard the doc. Let's go!" Brandon said.

He smooched her on the lips. "I'll be right back, babe!"

She didn't return the kiss, and when he saw her eyes open in shock, he knew he had overstepped his boundaries. "I'm sorry, Anna," he said. "We'll talk when I get back."

"I'll go to the room and pack up," she said.

Chapter 14

After the broadcast and back in his room, Jason stripped out of his bloodstained shirt and shoved it into a laundry bag with his other dirty clothes and crammed it into his duffle. He thanked his lucky stars he had one more clean shirt to wear for the ride back. His head throbbed as he strained to pick up his full bag. He'd probably have to deal with that for a few days until his cut started to heal. Making a doctor's appointment for Monday morning was his priority, just to make sure he wouldn't keel over in his sleep one night. He'd once read in a newspaper article that that could happen sometimes with head injuries, not that he doubted Anna's medical skills. By the looks of it, she'd cleaned him up pretty darn good, and he wanted to thank her for that.

Jason checked his hotel room to make sure he wasn't leaving anything behind, then brought his luggage and cooler downstairs to check out.

"Sir?" the receptionist called out.

He turned his head, and when he realized she meant him, he walked over to the counter. "Yes, ma'am?"

"Are you checking out?"

"Yes. We're heading back to Magnolia Hill," he said. "Why, is something wrong?"

"I'm afraid so," the receptionist said. ""Highway 80 going off the island is flooded and there's debris everywhere. It'll be at least until morning before it'll open up for traffic again. Would you like to stay another night?"

Jason nodded. "That'll be fine. I assume that there will be a discount?"

"Yes, sir. Our manager authorized a fifty percent discount for our guests while the power is out. You will see it on your final bill."

"Thank you. Can you also extend the stay for my team, Brandon Brewer and Anna Weaver?"

"Certainly," she replied. "I just need to reprogram your room keys."

Jason pulled his key card and the spare out of his pocket. As he handed her the keys, he glanced over to the hallway and noticed the exit signs were lit. He didn't notice it before, especially when his brain was still foggy early this morning. "You have power?"

She nodded. "We have a back-up generator for our computer system and other basic requirements but, unfortunately, it's not large enough to handle guest rooms."

"By chance, do you know if any of the other hotels have electricity?" he asked, but already knowing the answer.

"As far as I know, the entire island has lost power." She handed back his cards.

"Thank you anyway, for letting us stay another night," he said and tucked his cards back in his back pocket and dragged his luggage and cooler back up the stairs to his room. Actually, he was relieved to spend more time with

Anna. They needed to talk, and the highway closure was exactly what would give them time to work through whatever stood between them. At least he hoped so.

 Jason knocked at Brandon's door.

"Hey, man," Brandon said. "Are you heading out?"

"Nope. I have bad news, Brandon."

Brandon cocked his head. "What's up?"

"The highway is closed until at least tomorrow morning. We're kinda stuck here tonight."

Brandon's expression fell. "Figures. I was looking forward to go home to my girl."

"Sorry, but while we're here already, we might as well get more footage and do a few more broadcasts," Jason said. "I need to let Anna know that we're spending another night, then I'll call the station to give them an update. Let's meet in the lobby in thirty minutes. Oh, and don't forget to get your key card reprogrammed."

"All right, man. See you in a few," his friend said and closed the door.

Next, Jason walked to Anna's door. He lifted his hand to knock, when he heard a commotion on the other side and the door opened.

"Aaah!" Anna jumped back. "You scared the heck out of me. I didn't expect anybody standing in the hall."

"Sorry, I didn't mean to startle you," he said. "You might want to put those bags back in your room. It seems we're stuck on the island until tomorrow morning." He pointed at her luggage. "I already asked the receptionist to extend your stay for another night."

Her facial expression fell. "Oh?"

Jason wasn't sure if the poor living conditions or the extended trip with him caused Anna's disappointment. He rarely had seen her as upset with him as she was earlier at the beach.

"We have no power," she said.

A weight was lifted off his shoulders. She was worried about the hot room and lack of electricity and not so much about him. "Neither does the rest of Tybee, as I hear. Can I give you a hand with your bags?"

She shook her head. "No, it's okay. I don't want you to strain too much after that number that flying board did on you earlier." Anna pushed her luggage against the closet area in her room. "Come on in," she said and smiled at him, but he could tell the sparkle in her eyes was missing.

Yes, she was still upset, even though she tried to hide it. Standing awkwardly with his hands in his pocket in the middle of her room, he said, "Brandon and I are going to record some footage in a few minutes. Do you want to tag along?"

Anna looked around the room, then laughed at him. "You're kidding, right?"

He smiled at her, unsure if she was serious or sarcastic.

"Come on, Jason, you didn't think I was going to sit here in this hot, damp hotel room by myself doing nothing, did you?"

The snark in her tone surprised him. That didn't go well. "Of course not. I just wanted to give you the option, you know, in case you need some time to recover from the hurricane. It's not uncommon to feel exhausted after the effects of the adrenaline rush wear off. I've been in some dicey situations before, and after the danger was over and I was able to relax, I often struggled to stay alert on my drive back to the station." *For cryin' out loud, stop rambling*, Jason admonished himself.

"I'm sorry, Jason. I didn't mean to bite your head off," Anna said, lowering her head. "I think you're right, today is catching up with me." Then, with sudden newly found strength, her head shot up. "But I'm fine. Besides, you never know if someone might need medical attention. I bet first responders are spread thin right about now."

"You might be right. If you give me a minute, I'm going to call the station and let them know about the change of plans. Why don't you call Maggie and update her, and then we'll go do some exploring." Their talk would have to wait until later when their work was done.

Since Bessie boasted a nice hole in the passenger side of the windshield the 2x4 board left behind, the team decided on taking both vehicles.

Jason tossed Anna's medic bag in his truck and climbed into the driver's seat. He rolled down his window. "Be careful about downed trees and power lines," he told Brandon.

His friend gave him a thumbs up. "Lead the way, boss."

Jason put the key into the ignition but paused. He glanced at Anna and noticed she was running out of steam. "Are you sure you want to come along?"

She nodded. "Yes, I can't spend my day in the hotel room while someone on this island might need my help. This was a dangerous storm, and people get hurt..."

"Look, I'm sorry for putting you in danger earlier. I was so excited that my professionalism went out the window. I was wrong, and I don't blame you for being upset with me."

"Yeah, it was stupid," she said.

He ventured into an unsure smile. *This might take some work,* he thought. "I'm not sure how, but I want to make up for it somehow. I owe you big-time."

"Let's just go," she said.

In Anna terms, it meant this discussion was over for now. He put his truck into gear and let her be. Jason knew she was mad at him about that broadcast, but he still didn't know why she was acting different this morning. He'd have to give her some time. She always needed to think things through before she was ready to talk.

The roads were barely passable on the island. Tree limbs, building materials, and other large debris littered the road. Even though the storm surge didn't breach the dunes, some lower stretches of the road were covered in ponding water from the storm. Needless to say, their progress to find a suitable spot for filming was slow. Jason shook his head as he glanced into his rear-view mirror and saw Brandon navigating around obstacles and taking pictures out of his driver window at the same time. His friend was nuts.

They didn't get far before they saw a partially collapsed wooden house down the street. An elderly man was stumbling around and rummaging through the pile of wood and sheet rock that Jason assumed had once been his home.

"Stop the truck!" Anna said.

He pulled his vehicle into the man's driveway.

She got out as soon as the vehicle stopped moving. "Grab my bag for me, Jason, will you?"

Brandon parked Bessie by the sidewalk and ran to the home.

"Sir, are you okay?" Anna called out to the man as she limped toward the collapsed building.

"Help me! My wife is trapped in the house!" he said, continuing to move one board after the other out of the way. "Help me!"

Jason rushed toward them with the medical supplies. He dropped the bag on the wet ground.

"Sir, stop moving these boards. This house is not stable," Anna said. "If we move the wrong board, the whole front of the house could collapse and killing you and your wife."

"I have to get to her," the man said, not giving up.

"Sir, please have a seat on that piece of wall and let us take a look."

He didn't budge. "No, that's my wife in there."

"Please? Let us help you."

Jason saw Anna lead the old man to the wall. They had to find a way to get to his wife. "Hello? Can you hear me, ma'am?" he called out. "Talk to me so we can find you!" But there was no response.

"I think we might be able to clear a path into the house over here," Brandon suggested while pointing at a beam holding up a piece of roofing.

"Jason, try the back door," Anna called out.

Leave it to Anna. Why didn't he think of that sooner? "Come on, Brandon, maybe we can get to her from that side of the house."

They walked around the home and opened the back door, thankfully unlocked.

"Ma'am? Hello? Where are you?" Brandon called out.

"Shhh!" Jason said. "Did you hear that?" He paused. "Ma'am, call out again!"

He could hear her faint and muffled cry from the living room, which was partially collapsed.

"We're coming to you," Jason said. "Don't move!"

The building was unstable. The wooden floor creaked with every step. One wrong move could cause the walls and roof around them collapse onto them and onto the man's wife, killing them in an instant.

"I'm here," the woman said. He saw her hand waving from behind a partially opened closet door that held the ceiling up. A piece of the ceiling dangled in front of the closet, exposing wires, beams, and old insulation. The door was stuck, but they had to get this poor woman out of there.

"If we can brace the door frame, we might be able to move the closed door just enough to get her out," Brandon suggested.

Jason looked around. "See those two pieces of wood by the front door? They don't seem to hold anything up."

"On it," Brandon said.

Jason cringed with each moan of the floorboards as Brandon walked to the front of the house to retrieve the wood. He didn't dare breathe.

Brandon smiled as he turned.

Jason's heart stopped as a piece of the ceiling above Brandon fell with a loud swoosh to his feet, trailed by a plume of dust and insulation.

The old woman in the closet winced.

Brandon coughed. "I'm okay," he called out, then carried those pieces of wood to the door. "I have to admit, that was close."

Jason shook his head. "Let's try to make it out alive."

Careful not to disturb the door or any other beams, they jammed the boards under the closet door frame.

Jason prayed the rigged support would hold.

Together, the men shifted the closet door to make an opening wide enough for the woman to squeeze through and get her out the back door to safety.

"Ma'am, can you tell me where you're hurting?" Anna asked the pale and shaky woman.

"My wrist and my head hurt. Where's all that blood coming from?" she asked.

"You have a few cuts, but I can take care of those," Anna said. "You might have a broken wrist, and you have a big goose egg on the back of your head."

The woman looked at Jason. "Hey, aren't you the weatherman from Channel Ten?"

Flattered, he nodded and handed Anna the supplies she asked for as she worked on the woman's cuts. "Why didn't you two evacuate?" he asked out of curiosity.

"Oh, we've lived here all our lives," the man said. "We weren't going to let a bit of weather get the best of us, but this Gerard packed a bigger punch than we expected."

"That was quite a bit of weather you took on," Anna said.

Jason had heard similar stories from countless of survivors over the years who had refused to evacuate. Most of those staying behind were young locals, the invincible ones, who rode the storm out with hurricane parties. Others had lived through many hurricanes and became complacent. Many of those stories didn't have a happy ending.

He heard the diesel engine rumble of a larger vehicle approaching and turned toward the road. "It's an ambulance," he called out and flagged it down for them.

Anna caught up the medics on the elderly couple. "The patient's vitals are stable," she began. "She has a contusion on the back of her head, possibly a fractured wrist, and several lacerations. Other than that, I think Mrs. Klingensmith is doing great, considering the circumstances."

"Are you a doc?" one of the medics asked.

Anna shook her head. "Nah, paramedic. I just moved back to Magnolia Hill and am waiting on my license to be transferred from Colorado."

"Welcome back, then," the other medic said.

She watched them load the patient on the ambulance.

"Are you okay?" the medic asked. "You're limping."

"I'm fine. It's only a cut from the beach yesterday. I've cleaned and bandaged the wound and checked on it earlier. Just take care of this nice couple. I'll get our doc to take a look when we get back to Magnolia Hill."

Brandon set up his camera and got a shot of the ambulance driving away.

"So, what do you say, Jason? I think we should go live before other news stations swarm this place."

"Anna?" Jason gave her his most irresistible smile he could muster in hopes she'd approve another broadcast. Not that they needed it, but he didn't want to upset her even more today, especially if they were going to have their much-needed talk to clear the air between them.

Anna rolled her eyes. "As if you two would listen to what I have to say. Go on," she conceded.

Chapter 15

All afternoon, Anna was in her element helping people who were injured or in need because of the hurricane. She hadn't realized until now how much she had missed working as a paramedic. With any luck, her Georgia license would arrive in the mail soon so that she could find a job in the emergency medical services field again. She already had her resume ready to go. "So, Mr. Winterbottom, you're all patched up," she said helping him up, then turned to suppress a yawn. It'd been a long day.

She walked over to where Brandon and Jason finished another broadcast on the aftermath of the storm. "I'm out of supplies," she said to Jason once they'd finished. "I think it's time for me to turn in."

"And I'm starving," Brandon added.

Jason checked his watch. "It's about dinner time. I have more sandwich fixin's in the cooler." He pointed at the back of his truck. "This thermoelectric cooler is the best investment I've ever made."

"I second that," said Brandon, rubbing his belly.

Anna's stomach growled in response. She had been so distracted all day that she forgot to eat. Food sounded great right about now, but her body had other ideas in mind, such as getting to her room and crawling into bed. Every muscle ached, and her arms and legs dragged as if she had weights attached to them. Maybe a sandwich would give her enough energy to call home before she collapsed on her bed. "The hotel should have some plasticware we can use."

They climbed into their vehicles and drove back to the hotel.

Ten minutes later, they stood in front of their adjacent hotel room in the interior hallway of the second floor. Of course, the power was still out.

"Let's freshen up and meet in the breakfast area downstairs in about fifteen minutes," Jason suggested.

Anna was looking forward to splash cold water in her face and change into fresh clothes. "Sounds good," she said and swiped her card, but her lock wouldn't budge. Instead a red dot blinked. She let out a groan and tried again, but the she couldn't get it to unlock.

"What's wrong?" Jason asked.

"My card's not working," she said, still trying. The last thing she needed was to be locked out of her room with all her stuff inside. She was hungry, tired, and out of patience.

"My card's not working, either," Brandon said.

Jason tried his, and to add insult to injury, his worked. "Feel free to come in and use the restroom to freshen up. We can get the keys taken care of when we go downstairs to eat," he said. "The receptionist said earlier we should be good to go for another night. I'm sure it's just a matter of reprogramming the key cards."

Anna wasn't so sure. "I hope you're right, or we'll all be camping out in your room for the night."

"Don't worry, Anna, it'll be fine."

Jason's reassuring smile gave her hope that within the hour she'd be in her room, in bed, and snoozing.

A few minutes later and somewhat refreshed, the trio walked down to the reception desk with their room keys in hand.

"Ma'am," Anna said to the receptionist. "My card isn't working, and I'm locked out of my room. Can you give me a new one? I understand my stay was extended another night."

"Mine's not working, either," Brandon added.

"Yes, Mr. Morrisson did extend the reservation for another night, but unfortunately our card equipment stopped working about an hour ago. Our maintenance staff is spread thin making emergency repairs. I can try to track someone down with a master key to let you into your room."

"That'll be fine," Jason said to the receptionist. "We were planning to eat some sandwiches down here anyway. I'll go get the cooler, while you guys pick us a seat," he said to Anna and winked at her before heading through the busted door into the parking lot to get the food and water.

He looked as tired as she felt, but the small laugh lines around his eyes were still there, putting her at ease, letting her know that everything will be all right, regardless of how bleak their current situation seemed. Soon, someone would come to let her and Brandon into their rooms and she could finally rest for the night.

Jason returned with the cooler, and in less than half an hour, the sandwiches were gone. There were two more of Maggie's hardboiled eggs left on the table, and the men were eyeballing them.

"You aren't saving these for anything, are you?" Brandon asked Anna.

To be honest, she was tired of the eggs, especially after the peeling incident that morning. "Go ahead, Brandon, you can have them."

Brandon was about to take them both when Jason slapped his hand away from the other. "One of them is mine. Didn't your momma teach you how to share?"

"She said I could have them."

Anna giggled. Watching the two interact was like watching toddlers fighting over a toy. In the end, they duked it out over a game of rock paper scissors, and both got an egg.

After they cleaned up their mess, at last, one of the hotel employees approached them. "I understand you are locked out of your rooms?" the man asked.

Anna nodded. "Yes, sir." *Finally! Bed, here I come*, Anna thought.

"Follow me. I'll open them up for you," the employee said. "Once you're in, though, be sure not to lock yourself out again."

"I promise," Anna said and smiled at Jason as they took the stairs to their rooms.

The employee swiped his master key in front of Anna's lock. "Hmm. I don't understand. It won't open for me, either."

"You've got to be kidding!" Anna said.

"I'm sorry, but I'm not sure why this lock is not working. Something must've gone wrong when the room access system went down at the reception desk," the man said. "Let me try your room, sir," he said to Brandon, who stepped out of his way. He swiped the master key, and the red dot blinked again. "I don't understand. The only thing I can tell you is that we are trying to get the system downstairs working again, but it might take a while before we can get you back into your rooms."

"Thanks for trying, man," Brandon said, and the employee left to tend to other emergencies.

Jason turned to Anna. "If you want, you can have my room. Consider it as a thank you for saving our lives today. Brandon and I can sleep in the vehicles."

"That's silly. You have two queen-size beds in your room. We can all stay in it."

Brandon threw his hands in the air. "Nope, not happenin'. I'll spend the night in the van with air-conditioning."

"So that leaves you, Jason," she said. "I really don't mind sharing. Besides, it's yours anyway."

Jason raked his hands through his hair. "Only if you don't mind. I can always sleep in the truck."

Anna smiled. "It's fine. There are two beds."

"All right, then. I'll stay," Jason said.

Brandon did a one-eighty and held his hand up with a half-shake. "On that happy note, I'm outta here," he said. "See you in the morning."

She wasn't so sure it was a good idea to share a room with Jason again after last night. All afternoon she had avoided the uncomfortable conversation she was certain she had to face sooner or later. Later was fine with her because she dreaded having to crush Jason's hopes the way he had crushed hers in high school. Now that they were alone, she couldn't run from the inevitable talk any longer.

Anna accepted the spare T-shirt from Jason before she stepped into the bathroom. She struggled to keep her eyes open but forced herself to take a cold shower to get the grime off her in hopes it would give her another energy boost, but it wasn't meant to be. She was running on empty.

As she dried off and slipped the shirt over she head, she was painfully aware that they were alone now. They would have to talk tonight, but she didn't even have enough strength left to even think about it. Every muscle in her body ached from tensing up in fear during the worst of the storm. She was done for the day.

"Feel better?" Jason asked with a smile as she walked to the bed.

She shook her head. "I'm so done." In slow motion, Anna peeled back the comforter that no doubt hadn't been washed in weeks and let it slide onto the floor. It was still hot in the room. All she wanted was to crawl under the remaining flat sheet and fall asleep.

With eyes half shut, she watched as Jason nonchalantly stripped down to his boxer briefs and then closed the bathroom door to take his shower. *Too bad this all has to end,* she thought and turned around.

Her phone buzzed. She checked the display. It was Maggie. Oh no, she'd been so preoccupied earlier she'd forgotten to check in. Thanks to her battery packs and the USB plugs in Jason's truck, she had an almost full charge. "Hey, Mom," she said, stifling a yawn. "Is everything okay?"

"Yes, darling, everything is fine over here. We have some flooding in town, but we're safe. I heard they are about to close a few roads. The news said there was an accident on the county road leading out of town earlier today. They didn't say who it was yet, but you know how word spreads around here."

Anna could only hope that whoever was in the wreck was okay. "What about the kids?"

"Honey, the girls are having a blast making more bracelets, and Sean picked Grady up a little while ago." She paused. "More importantly, how are you holding up?"

"Oh, Mom, I don't know what to do," she said, her voice shaky. She didn't want to cry.

"I have a feeling this is not about the hurricane anymore. Is it Jason?"

Anna took a deep breath. "Yes," she whispered, afraid Jason could hear her. "This is all moving so fast. It feels like we've never been apart, but we've both been through so much. What if this is just a rebound?"

"Anna, I think deep inside you know what the right answer is, and you already know I think you two are soulmates. But only you can decide for yourself what to do. My only advice is to follow your heart."

She sighed. "You're right, but everything seems too perfect, like the other shoe is about to drop."

"Like I said, honey, I don't think you have anything to worry about with Jason. He's nothing like Luke, and I'm sure you already know that." Maggie paused, then continued. "Whatever you decide to do, I will always support you, kiddo."

"Thanks, Mom." Anna yawned loud enough for Maggie to hear. "Sorry, I'm exhausted. Tell Ash we'll be home tomorrow. I'll call you in the morning before we head out. Good night, Mom."

"Good night, kiddo," Maggie said and hung up.

Suddenly, the phone felt heavy in her hand, and it wasn't because of the battery pack. She sat it on the nightstand and laid back, staring at the popcorn ceiling. She closed her eyes. What was she going to do? Spending time with Jason was wonderful. He made her feel young and carefree again. The decades that had separated them only seemed like months now. During this trip, all she wanted was to spend every single moment with him. She had to admit, she had a serious crush on him, and the way he winked at her before broadcasts made it even worse.

It's just nostalgia, the voice in her head said, bursting her juvenile happiness bubble in one giant pop. Was the magic between Jason and her simply familiarity? It could be. He's a celebrity. Why would he want someone like you? the internal voice, sounding so similar to Luke's, taunted her. Deep inside, she had hoped that her divorce would be the end of all her Luke troubles. Yet, the scars remained, the deep scars Luke had carved into her soul over the years—she wasn't good enough. What if it was true? Jason deserved someone better than her. Someone who could cook. Someone who wore a size ten instead of a twenty. Someone who didn't doubt herself with everything she did. How could she love someone if she couldn't even love herself for who she was? How could she love him wholeheartedly when doubt and negative thoughts constantly preoccupied her mind? Any romantic relationship with her would be doomed, no matter how much she wanted to be with Jason. In the long run it was easier to end it now before they let themselves get too deep.

Anna curled up in bed and pulled the sheet to her chin. All she wanted to do was cry into her pillow, fall asleep, and wake up to a world without worries. Anna knew that that wouldn't happen.

Jason joined her on her bed. "Hey, what's up, darling? Is the day catching up with you?"

She was so tempted to wrap her arms around him and seek protection from the world and her ex, despite the sticky heat in the room, but she didn't.

Jason put a hand on her shoulder.

She didn't dare turn around to look into his sad eyes. If she did, she couldn't guarantee that she would be able to resist falling into his arms.

"Tell me what's on your mind, Anna," he said with a soft voice and stroked her shoulder.

She had hoped she could avoid this moment, but she couldn't hold back any longer. She took a deep breath, exhaled, then turned toward him. His face blurred behind her unshed tears.

He had his head propped on one hand, and as she feared, her resolve began to crumble. But she had to be strong. It wasn't fair to lead him to believe there was hope for them. It wasn't fair to him. She had to end their relationship, if you could even call that, before it was too late. It was for his own good. "Jason, we came here as friends," she began.

"Okay," he said. "There's no rush, baby. Let's just spend more time together and take it slow. We can take all the time we need."

She shook her head. "We can't, Jason! We just can't..." The tears spilled down her face, and she couldn't stop them any longer.

"Anna, don't do this! I love you!" he pleaded.

Her mind was racing with all the reasons why she decided they couldn't be together. "It's for the best."

"Why?"

"I've changed, Jason. I'm not the same as I was in high school. You deserve someone...someone better than me," she sobbed.

His eyes narrowed, and his hand gripped her arm. "Look at me, Anna. Don't you ever let anyone tell you you're not good enough. Do you understand? You are perfect as you are. I love you!"

Anna flinched and pushed herself away from him toward the headboard.

He let go of her arm. "No, no, no! I'm sorry! I'm so sorry! It's me, babe, Jason. I'd never hurt you!"

She covered her face with her hands. Her throat ached.

"It was that bad?"

She nodded.

"What happened?"

Anna paused, not sure if she should open up to him, but Jason had always been a good listener, and she knew he was genuinely worried. She took a deep breath. "I had a tough call on New Year's Eve. A guy had stabbed his wife and teenage daughter over something trivial. We got them to the hospital in time, but for the rest of my shift, I kept thinking of what happened to them. I knew it was just a matter of time when Luke would lose his temper again, and the ambulance would have to come for Ash and me instead."

"He hurt you before?"

Anna nodded. "Most of the time he was just yelling, shoving, and getting into my face. That night, he didn't hold back."

Jason raked his fingers through his hair. "Oh, Anna."

Now that the dam was breached, the words spilled out like a raging river. She had to tell her story. There was no stopping. "I came home early from my shift. My head was still spinning from that call earlier that night. I caught him cheating in our living room, Jason. He was so mad that I came home early that he choked me until I lost consciousness. The next thing I remember is waking up in an ambulance." She shuddered.

"I'm so sorry that happened to you."

She paused, then continued. "He wasn't always like that. He changed and became jealous and controlling over everything I did. It got worse the longer he worked in law enforcement and the higher he climbed on the career ladder. He'd seen a lot of bad stuff."

"But that's no excuse, Anna. You know that."

"I do, but it was complicated. The cost of living is so high in Colorado Springs, I couldn't afford to leave Luke. Worst yet, I didn't want to lose Ashleigh to him. Now do you see?"

He tentatively took one hand from her face and gently pulled her to him. "Anna, baby, it breaks my heart to see you hurt like that."

She leaned on his chest as he held her tight, rocking her.

"I don't know how you got the idea into your head that you're not good enough," he said a few minutes later. "I've known you since we were kids sitting on that rotten tree and spitting cherry pits into the creek. If I'm not mistaken, there are two full-grown cherry trees just a quarter mile downstream."

"There are not!"

"Well, it might be pine trees. Either way, what I'm trying to say is that I know the real you. Whatever it is you need to work through, let me be a part of this," he said.

She shook her head. "Don't make this any harder than it needs to be, please?" Her heart broke when she saw the disappointment in his eyes. "Jason, I have to do get my own life together before I can let anyone else into my life. I'm a mess, and I'm scared of getting hurt again if things don't work out with us."

What she really wanted to do was kiss his soft lips again and lose herself in his arms, but the nagging voice in her head was telling her to be rational. Her heart was aching, both for what she had to give up and for breaking Jason's heart. She had gotten a reminder last night of how things used to be between them and how they could be again. She had gotten his hopes up, leading him on to believe that they would have a future together—their happy ever after. No, they couldn't. Not now. "We came here as friends, remember?"

"That was the deal." He raked his free hand through his hair. "I'm sorry for overstepping my boundaries last night. I just thought…"

"Maybe we were both excited about the hurricane." *And reliving our youth*, she added in her mind. "Friends?" she offered with an uneasy smile.

There was a long silence. "If that's what you want, Anna, I'll take it.

Friends. We should get some sleep. It's been a long day," he said as he got up and moved to the other bed. "Good night, Anna."

As if on cue, his insides rumbled. "Sorry about that," he said, rubbing his belly.

Anna wrinkled her nose, hoping that wasn't a sign of worse things to come tonight. "Good night," she replied.

Now that the truth was out and the air between them was clear, why didn't she feel any better about her decision?

Her face was puffy and swollen, and her nose was clogged. That was the last thing she remembered before falling into a deep slumber.

Chapter 16

No matter what he did, Jason could not fall asleep. It was too hot, and his mind was spinning faster than the rotating winds of an EF4 twister. He knew it was hopeless to force sleep to come. Anna was just within reach beside him and yet still too far away. The rumbling and twisting inside of his gut didn't make it any easier on him, either. It must have been those dang boiled eggs he had for dinner.

Jason heard a faint snore escaping from Anna. If he wasn't able to sleep, he might as well try to process what happened this weekend between him and Anna. Forget the hurricane.

What started out as a great idea of catching up after God dropped a hurricane into his lap ended in disaster. It all started so innocently, until the moment he raced her on the beach after that first broadcast yesterday afternoon. Divine intervention or not, who was he kidding when he'd said that they could go chase a hurricane as friends? *There you go, Jason,* he thought. *You should've known better than trying to relive old memories.* What should've been a fun and exciting weekend left Anna upset and him guilty for ruining the trip.

His gut rumbled and cramped up again. Was this digestive

disagreement his punishment for not trying harder to practice some sort of restraint around her? He definitely crossed an invisible boundary the moment he kissed Anna on the forehead. The moment his lips had touched her skin, he was a goner, even though he knew he shouldn't have even let it get that far. Even worse, he went back to her room where they fell asleep in each other's arms.

Another cramp twisted his insides. Darn eggs. At least feeling rotten inside distracted him from his beautiful friend lying in the other bed beside him, fast asleep.

His thoughts drifted to Caroline. He could see her in his mind as if she was standing right in front of him. Her facial expression told him she was worried.

The stabbing pain of guilt returned, along with the memories of last night. He had made a promise to Caroline, and he had broken that promise last night when he'd kissed Anna. Maybe he had misinterpreted the notion of Caroline releasing him. What if it was plain old wishful thinking he had experienced? It wouldn't have been the first time Caroline had to spell things out for him. Was her perceived presence last night just his mind trying to justify what he really wanted to do? Jason had always been a man of integrity and loyalty. Right now he didn't think he had displayed either of those qualities. Was he really ready to let go of her? He wasn't so sure. Even though Caroline had passed two years ago, he still felt as if he betrayed her. Blood rushed to his head, making his wound throb. What had he done? He was such a fool—a selfish fool.

As he spiraled down the path of doubt and guilt, Caroline's sad eyes lifted as if to give him hope. Love flooded his mind and pushed his self-defeating thoughts out of his head. With these thoughts, Caroline also began to fade.

"Wait!" he called out in his mind. He wanted to hold on to her, hold on to her memory. He had so much left to say to her. Instead, she winked at him and disappeared. She was a kind soul. What would she say, if she could talk to him right now? Deep inside he knew. All she would want for him was to be happy, but instead, his sense of loyalty got in his way, making him feel weak and like a failure.

Whatever he felt didn't matter anymore, because Anna already friend zoned him, as his daughter Sarah would say. The more he thought about it, it was for the best. She needed to deal with her trauma, and he wasn't ready to let go of Caroline. With his gut cramping, he stumbled to the bathroom. It would be a miracle if he survived the night.

* * *

The next morning, Brandon knocked on their hotel room door. "Good morning, sleeping beauties, the roads are open, and they fixed the room key machine," he said. "And, man, I had the runs from hell last night. Did anybody else get sick?"

Anna got a whiff of a rather strange scent, to be polite, emanating from Brandon. He must have really had a rough night. Anna thanked her lucky stars that they were riding home in separate vehicles.

"You're oversharing, Brandon," Jason said, "and, yes, my gut was twisting in ways I never thought it could."

 "Serves you two right for being so greedy with those eggs." Anna regretted her answer the moment the words had left her lips.

"Whoa, Anna! What's up? Did Jason snore too loud again?"

"I'm sorry, Brandon. I think I need some coffee."

She could see Brandon and Jason's nonverbal gestures from the corner of her eye. She deserved that. All she wanted at this point was to get home and forget about the rest of the world. Anna still felt bad for disappointing Jason last night. She was also upset about how much power Luke still had over her. They were divorced, yet he still haunted her. When would it end? It was her fault that the air between her and Jason was thick as Mamaw's special mashed potato soup. And now she had to deal with the outcome, uncomfortable as it may be.

"Well," Brandon said, interrupting her private pity party, "I'll freshen up and leave you guys to it. My girlfriend can't wait for me to get home." He winked, and with a spring in his step, he walked over to his room door and unlocked it.

After Jason got Anna's key reprogrammed at the front desk, Anna took a quick shower in her room and slipped into some cleaner clothes for the trip home. They loaded their bags into the truck.

Brandon was already in the parking lot about to take off.

"Have a safe trip back to Savannah," Anna said as Brandon climbed into the battered storm tracker vehicle.

He gave her a thumbs up. "It was a pleasure to meet you, Anna." Brandon closed the door and rolled down the driver's side window. "By the way," he said, pointing back and forth at them. "It's none of my business, but whatever it is you guys are squabbling about, you need to work it out. Seriously, you're wasting all this time overthinking things, when instead, you could have had the time of your lives with this hurricane." He shook his head. "Like I said, it's none of my business." With that, he waved at them one last time and drove off.

At first, Anna wasn't sure if she should feel offended by what Brandon said. True, her relationship with Jason wasn't any of his concern. Was he right, though? They had the opportunity of a lifetime to witness extreme weather, something they both were passionate about. She turned toward Jason.

He met her gaze for a painful moment, then broke eye contact and lowered his ball cap. "It's mighty sunny out this morning," he said, shifting his point of gravity from one leg to the other. He sighed. "Look, I'm sorry this weekend went south."

"We were in the eye of the hurricane, though," she said and attempted a smile. Anna couldn't bear looking at him. The first night, where they had fallen asleep in each other's arms, was wonderful. Now that Gerard was skirting the Carolinas as a tropical storm, and their relationship was over, there wasn't much left to say. "Well, I think I've had enough excitement this weekend. Are you ready to head home?"

He nodded and got into the driver's seat of his truck.

Jason and Anna drove across the island in silence. She watched as they passed families milling around to assess damage and clear debris Gerard left on their properties. Some of the older houses they passed had missing roofs or broken windows. Other properties in lower-lying areas still had water puddling in yards. Some families would have a long road of recovery ahead of them—and so would she. As soon as she had health insurance again, she'd start therapy to get well.

As they drove on, neither one wanted to address the obvious.

Jason broke the silence when they got on the highway toward Savannah. "What's on your mind?" he asked.

She stared out the window and watched the trees zoom by. "I don't know," she replied. He didn't press the issue, and for that she was thankful.

"I did a lot of thinking last night," he said after another moment of awkward silence.

Anna dared a curious glance at him, then turned away. She didn't want him to see the tears that were puddling in her eyes, ready to breach the dam once again.

"I think we've made the right decision. It's for the best that we stay as friends. It's too soon for me, too," he admitted.

Even if it hurt, ending where they were headed was the logical thing to do. She had to suck up her feelings of loss of what they could've had and disappointing Jason and get over them. It had been her decision, and she had to be okay with it.

"When first I saw you," he said. "I felt like I was back in high school again. I wanted to make up for the decades we had missed. In reality, I'm not sure I'm ready. Gosh, Anna, when I ran into you at the park, I wondered if one day we would start over. I guess it's not that easy, is it?"

Anna shook her head, then continued looking out of the window. She wiped the tears off her cheek with the back of her hand, hoping he wouldn't see her cry. Why was she so miserable and sad? Logically, she made the right decision. Emotionally, it still hurt.

They drove in silence the rest of the way home. The agony was only interrupted by the classic rock station playing breakup songs that were worse than some country songs she had ever heard over the years.

A few minutes out from the house, Jason called Sarah's number via voice command. "Hey, honey," he said when she answered.

His daughter's voice sounded over the truck speakers. "Hey, Dad."

"We'll be home in about five minutes. Can you meet me at the door?"

Sarah paused for a moment. "Uh, Dad, is everything okay?"

"Yes, sweetie," he said. "I'm just running late and...never mind."

"Okay, I'll pack my stuff and see you in a few minutes."

Jason disconnected the call.

He dropped Anna off, talking only to Maggie and Sarah when it was necessary.

Maggie gave him and Anna a good look over. "Something you wanna tell me?"

"Thank you, Maggie, for letting Sarah stay with you," he said.

"You're welcome, but that's not what I meant."

Jason sighed. "It's been a long weekend."

Maggie nodded. "Uh-huh," she said, then looked at Anna.

She knew that her mom wouldn't let it rest. "Later, Mom," she said. "I'm exhausted."

"Take care," Jason said with a sad frown on his face, letting his head hang for a moment before driving off.

Anna wasn't in the mood to talk and catch up. It took every ounce of determination not to fall apart in front of her mom and her daughter. "I have to take a nap," she half-sobbed, then disappeared into her room, sharing a good cry with her pillow and drenching it.

After, she didn't know how long she had wept, but she was all cried out. Anna rubbed her eyes, blew her nose, then just stared at the wall. A knock ripped her out of her numb state.

"Anna, darling, may I come in?"

"Yes, Mom." She wiped the last of her tears with her bedsheet, which had to get washed, anyway. "Come on in."

Maggie entered the room and sat down next to her on the bed. "Oh, honey, what happened? Are you ready to talk about it?"

Anna shook her head. She didn't want to retell her story yet. She couldn't. It still hurt too much.

"Is it about Jason?"

Anna nodded. "Mom, I don't know what to do."

Maggie drew her in her arms. "It's okay, honey, we'll get through this, too. You just let me know when you're ready to talk."

Once more, the tears were flowing freely, and for a moment, she felt safe and loved again.

Chapter 17

"Dad?" Sarah asked in the truck. "Is everything okay?"

Jason nodded. "Yes, sweetheart. Don't worry about me. Everything is fine. Tell me about your weekend!" He hoped for a recount of the hurricane, but his daughter was more impressed with the projects they were working on than with the monster of a storm on their front step.

"Look, Dad," Sarah said and held her wrist in front of him, showing off her red friendship bracelet. The words DRINK & were written in black and crossed out and DRIVE was written in white. "These are the bracelets we made," she said proudly. "It's my don't drink and drive design," she explained. She then held up another light pink one with a red heart and the word MOM worked into the knots. "And this one is a special bracelet to keep Mom close to me," she said, turning the band so that the writing rested centered on top of her wrist.

"They are beautiful, Sarah," Jason said, and he meant it.

"Ashleigh is really good with designing the statement templates. Not bad for a skater girl." She grinned and took a bite of her apple. "We decided to teach a class at the yarn shop to other teens to bring the younger crowd into the store. Maggie needs help." Sarah rolled her eyes.

"Seriously, Dad, nobody crochets potholders anymore! We stayed up all night during the storm and made these bracelets. Grady made some with a half-pipe design and skater stuff. We'll make more and sell them on consignment. Ash and I already worked out a deal with Maggie. We're going to try to spread the word in school, too," she rattled on, barely catching her breath.

He smiled at her rambling. It had taken her two years, but Sarah had gotten out of her shell and made a good friend. Ashleigh was the glue that brought all three of them together. The only trouble now was that her best friend was Anna's daughter. That meant there was no getting around talking to Anna. As Sarah would say, "Awkward!"

Sarah stopped talking. "Dad!" she called out. "Hello? Are you listening?"

They rolled into their driveway. "Yes, honey. I'm sorry, kiddo. My head's aching," he said. He wasn't sure if that was an excuse for tuning Sarah out, or if last night's talk was to blame for his depressed mood. "Maybe after I take a shower and a nap, I'll be better company."

"Dad, I totally saw how you got whacked on the head," she said excitedly. Then, as if she realized what could've happened, she chastised him. "What were you trying to prove, staying out in the weather like that?"

Jason winced by the volume of her voice. He stopped the truck in front of his garage and put it in park. "Oh, sweetheart, if you don't mind, let's talk later," he said, pressing his hand against his temple.

"I'm sorry, Dad. I didn't mean to yell," she said. "I just got really scared.

We've already lost Mom, and I don't know what would happen to me if you got killed, too. I need you."

"Sweetheart, I'm sorry, too. I didn't mean to scare you." He stretched his arm out to her and attempted to draw her into a one-armed hug, which deemed difficult with the console between their seats. Instead, he tucked a strand of her hair behind her ear and stroked her cheek as he had done so many times before when she was upset. "I got careless, and it was a stupid thing to do. What I should've done was following my own advice and taken shelter when the eyewall passed and the wind kicked up. I assure you this will never, ever, happen again." He lifted her chin. "I promise.'

The corners of her mouth lifted into a tentative smile. "That's okay, Dad. I just don't want to lose you, too," she said.

The gravity of her fear hit him like a freight train. He was her only parent, and he had put his life in danger. Jason felt like a jerk for not thinking things through. Suddenly, it all became clear. He had to start passing on the dangerous assignments to his younger, single meteorologists. It was time. How could he not see it before? "Sweetie, I'll be around and a pain in your neck until you're well into your eighties."

She chuckled followed by a yawn. "I think I could use another nap, too. We've had so much fun at Maggie's, and now it's catching up to me. Can you open the garage door for me?"

He did as she asked.

Sarah got out of the truck and grabbed her small suitcase from the back.

By the time he unloaded the truck and took a shower, Sarah was already passed out in her room. A nap sounded very appealing right about now—no, it was absolutely necessary.

He laid down on his bed and replayed the last two days in his head. To his surprise, or maybe not, Anna was again the focus of his thoughts, not the hurricane. Not that he picked them. Jason was torn. His lost love had returned and by overstepping his boundaries, he had managed to ruin what could've been a nice friendship with Anna. Now, things were extremely awkward between them. Worse, the guilt of thinking of Anna instead of Caroline was gnawing at him. Even though she had been gone for two years, he still had her picture beside his bed and talked to her every night before going to sleep. Worst of all, his antics this weekend had scared the bejesus out of Sarah. Was that all he was good for, letting down the people he loved?

Jason tossed and turned and couldn't find peace. He quietly called out to Caroline, asking for advice. She didn't answer. Instead, he heard a stirring outside of his bedroom door and a soft knock. "Dad?"

"Yes, sweetheart?" He sat up in his bed.

"Do you like Ashleigh's mom?" she asked, walked to him, and sat down next to him.

"Well, I do. We've been friends since high school. Why do you ask?"

She snuggled up to him. "I like her a lot, and Ashleigh and I are close like sisters. I miss Mom, but…"

He knew where this conversation was

going. "Listen, Sarah, I'm glad you like them..."

"They are like family already. Maggie is like a grandma to me."

"Oh, honey," he said and stroked her head.

She turned her head to look at him. "Did you have a fight?"

"No, we're friends."

"What happened? You looked so happy together."

"Sarah, it's complicated, and you shouldn't have to worry about my problems." The last thing he wanted for his daughter was to slip into the role of caretaker. He sensed that something was bothering Sarah, so he waited for her to continue.

"Dad?"

"Yes?"

"We would make a great family, wouldn't we?" Sarah said, twisting her friendship bracelet. "Ashleigh and I would be sisters, and you'd have someone to cuddle with at night."

"It's not that easy, sweetie, and since when have you grown up so much?"

Sarah smiled and left the room—and him to think.

The first thoughts were about Caroline, a happy Caroline. As he imagined her in his mind, the same peace he had experienced in the hotel room enveloped him. He just let the images come. He saw her gentle as always. "It's okay," she said. "I want you to be happy. I'm okay."

Jason turned the golden familiar wedding band on his left ring finger a few times. As if it was a sign, it seemed to move more easily than before. He turned it again, this time with an upward motion. To his surprise, the ring came off effortlessly. He held the engraved band in his hand. "You will always have a special place in my heart, Caroline," he said and put the ring in the top drawer of his dresser.

So this is what peace feels like? he wondered, and knew that everything would be okay now, no matter how many curveballs life threw him or how complicated things got.

Anna woke with the sun shining in her face and the fan whirling on the ceiling above her. She tried to focus on it, but her eyes were swollen from the night before. She checked her phone on the nightstand. Ugh, almost noon already? Why hadn't Maggie woken her? Last night she had decided that throwing herself into work would distract her from her heartache, even if it was of her own making. Her to-do list for the remodel had enough projects to keep her busy for a year. She hadn't got off to a good start today. Oh well!

She rubbed her eyes and noticed that the ceiling fan had blown half of the tear-and-snot-filled pile of tissues to the floor. With a deep breath and a sigh, she made herself get up, picked up the tissues, and threw them in the trash on the way to the shower. Maybe the warm water would wash away the grief that had left a void around her heart.

It didn't.

Her stomach was rumbling. Had she eaten last night? She couldn't remember. Anna poured a cup of coffee from the half-full pot when she noticed a sticky note on the fridge. She peeled it off the door and read.

Anna,

Went to the shop. I hope you had a good night's sleep. Didn't have the heart to wake you. Breakfast is in the fridge if you're hungry. The paint for the window frames and the door arrived Friday. Dress down if you still want to help. I'm leaving Woofus at home today so he won't leave tail-wagging patterns on the fresh paint. Take your time...

Love,

Mom

Anna sat the note aside and opened the refrigerator. A pile of pancakes sat covered on the middle shelf of the well-stocked fridge, but nothing appealed to her. She sipped the lukewarm coffee and plopped down on a chair. Her stomach was still urging her to eat, and so was the pulsing void in her chest. Thinking of Jason and how their weekend had gone from bliss to devastation, in more than one way, made her feel even worse.

A copy of the Magnolia Hill Times sat on top of the table. She groaned when she saw the picture plastered on the front page. It was Jason getting knocked over by the sheet of plywood on the beach. Yet, she couldn't resist and pulled the paper closer. She had to admit, the photo almost looked comical. Never mind that Gerard's flying debris could have killed all three of them that day. "Let's see what they wrote about us," she said to Woofus, who lifted his head.

Category 2 Hurricane to Blame for Injury Gone Viral

By Miriam Sue Webster

Tybee Island. *Coverage of Hurricane Gerard went viral this weekend after a local weatherman was struck and rendered unconscious by flying debris.*

Magnolia Hill's very own chief meteorologist, Jason Morrison, was on assignment to cover the arrival of Category 2 Hurricane Gerard Saturday morning. Morrison was demonstrating the rapid change of wind speed in the eyewall, when he and his cameraman, Brandon Brewer, were struck by a flying sheet of plywood. Both were knocked down and suffered head injuries.

The camera continued broadcasting as Colorado paramedic Anna Weaver provided medical care for the news team. Recordings of the broadcast went viral on social media and received worldwide news attention. Morrison: "Again, this proves that everyone should heed local weather warnings. Do not underestimate the power of nature. We were extremely lucky that day." Both Morrison and Brewer are expected to make a full recovery.

Paramedic Anna Weaver is the daughter of Maggie Weaver, owner of the Spinning Yarns craft shop on Main Street. The shop is currently undergoing renovations and a grand reopening is planned in the next few weeks.

* * *

Anna held the paper up. "Did you see this, Woofus? My name is in the paper, and the shop is getting free press."

The hound just grunted and looked at his empty food bowl.

"Okay, I get it," she said with mock disappointment, and got up to refill his bowl with kibbles. "At least someone has an appetite."

She gulped down the rest of her coffee. Wallowing in her emotions all day wouldn't exactly improve the appearance of her mom's shop. She had to get over Jason and figure out how to use this weekend's experience to better her current situation. Anna was determined to make a good life for herself and Ashleigh. Today marked a new day in chapter 2.0 of her new life. "I've got this!" she said and grabbed her purse.

The air was cool for August, thanks to Hurricane Gerard. She got into her Camry and dodged a few leftover tree branches on the road leading downtown. The restaurant's parking lot was full. Maybe there was parking around the block. As she passed a few businesses on Main Street, an elderly couple left the Cherry on Top Cupcake Shop and got into a car parked right in front of the shop. It took the couple a moment to get situated, so Anna turned on her blinker and waited.

Her gaze landed on the giant cupcake sign with the signature cherry on top of the icing and drifted down to the mint colored door and window frame. The large window showcased a tree of various cupcakes as the centerpiece. White satin material Jenna had draped over the display surface gave the appearance that her trays of cupcakes sat on a cloud of icing. Just looking at the cheerful storefront made her troubles evaporate into thin air, at least for the time being.

As soon as she pulled in and unbuckled her seatbelt, Jenna walked out of the store, wearing a ruffled pink apron and wiping her forehead with her arm. She looked exhausted.

"Rough day?" Anna asked as she got out and locked the car door. Locking her vehicle was a habit she acquired after she moved to the city to attend college. Within the first week away from home, someone already went through her car and stole her favorite CDs. Even though Magnolia Hill was safe, she didn't want to tempt fate again.

"The town is still full of evacuees, and I've been working nonstop to keep up with the baking. I'm almost sold out again, but..." She led Anna into her shop.

Anna could barely keep up with her friend. "I have a feeling I'll like where we're going."

They entered the kitchen. "I just

finished a batch of my Hurricane Caramel Swirl cupcakes."

Anna's eyes grew wide. "Are you kidding me?" On the table in front of her sat a plate with a batch of cupcakes made of white cake batter and wrapped in blue paper cups. White icing with gray swirls topped the pastries. "Oh, look at those cute fishies!" She bent down to inspect the different sea creatures that where attached to toothpicks and stuck out of the cupcakes.

"Go ahead! Take one!" Jenna said and handed her a napkin. "Cappuccino?"

"Yes, please!"

Anna pulled out a stool from under the table and sat on its edge. First, she peeled the paper off the cupcake. Caramel touched the edges of the paper. "Oh my!"

"It's called Caramel Swirl for a reason."

She bit into the cupcake, and the moist caramel in the dough set off her bliss receptors. "This is heaven!" she said, eyes closed. "You have to make us some of these for our grand opening."

"I'd love to." Jenna joined her with the cappuccinos and nudged her with her right shoulder. "Speaking of heaven and swirly hurricanes," she said. "I've been following the storm coverage. So"—she drew out the O. "Are you..." She hesitated. "You know, you and Jason?"

Anna almost choked on her cupcake. So much for her attempt to forget about him. Pictures of him flashed through her mind. Last night's pain caught up with her, and she fought back tears. Not again!

"Oh, no, sweetie pie!" Jenna sat down her cappuccino and embraced Anna. "I'm so sorry. What happened?"

"We went hurricane chasing as friends," she began, her voice cracking. "Then we kissed." She kept the rest of the night's details to herself.

"That's great news! So why are you crying?"

"I told him I wasn't ready for a relationship, and neither was he."

"Why?"

Anna recounted all the reasons why they couldn't be together.

"Really? That's all you've got?"

"What do you mean?" Anna was confused. "I need a new relationship right now like I need a hole in my head." She'd seen her share of bullet holes working as a paramedic, and it wasn't pretty.

Jenna pulled out a chair for herself and sat. "Do you love him?"

Anna hesitated, then nodded.

"Does he love you?"

She hung her head. "I don't know."

"Well, don't you want to find out?"

Chapter 18

The thick white paint filled the cracks of the old wooden window frame of the shop, only leaving behind smooth indentions as it dried. Leaving Colorado, Anna had felt like the cracked wood inside, but coming home had given her hope. She needed to be around loved ones more than ever, especially after what she had endured.

"Don't you want to find out?" Jenna's words had haunted her ever since she'd left her friend's shop, yet she couldn't gather the courage to call Jason. In her mind, it was clear that having a relationship was too soon for him. Besides, if he'd had a change of heart, he would have called her by now. She'd be better off continuing with her original plan of getting on her own two feet before she made any additional major life changes.

Anna patched a few more thin spots on the window frame and stepped off the ladder to admire her work. By now, the paint on the door had already dried. Amazing what a difference a fresh coat of paint could make. Tomorrow after skateboard practice, Ashleigh could work on the lettering.

Anna collapsed her ladder and stored it in the utility shed behind the shop. Ready to get out of the heat, she grabbed her bucket of paint and supplies and carried them inside the store. The cool air in the shop was refreshing. All she needed now was a tall glass of sweet tea and a few minutes to recuperate from the heat outside before she would tackle the next task on her long list of to-dos.

She walked over to the fridge, poured herself a tall glass of tea, and sat at one of the craft tables in the shop. The cold liquid did wonders for her thirst. As she rested, she looked around and admired their hard work they'd completed so far. Instead of the dreadful dark green, the walls around the yarn shelves were now a pleasant light blue, and the grayed over time molding and trim had a fresh coat of white satin paint. They also replaced the old and forgotten eighties advertisements for Maggie's popular yarn brands with fresh posters displayed in modest frames. The next big job would be to give the long-neglected hardwood floor some tender loving care and give it back its natural beauty.

They had already put countless long days into giving Spinning Yarns a facelift, and with time, the shop was getting its original charm back. Even better, the newly decorated window display with a few modern knit and crochet projects, such as baby booties, beautiful throws, and rolls of yarn spilling out of wooden baskets onto a white satin backdrop drew curious townspeople into the store to have a look. Most walked out inspired, with a ball of yarn or ten.

Anna was excited about the sudden interest in crafts. To her surprise, even some teenagers had stopped by the store after school yesterday asking for statement bracelets. The girls were having trouble keeping up with production, so they'd created a flyer with additional class dates for Anna and Maggie to hand out to customers.

Tonight was the girls' first time teaching their bracelet class. Anna couldn't be any prouder of them.

 Since the skateboarding competition was this Saturday, Anna decided to help the girls with prepping for their special evening. They expected a full class of fifteen students, and they barely had enough room to accommodate them. Between the occasional customers visiting the shop, she set out a variety of colorful balls of crochet yarn, scissors, and other supplies on the large wooden table. Maggie had found the table in a PennySaver ad for almost nothing and had someone from church deliver it yesterday. It was perfect for the craft nook. For now, the plastic chairs would have to do, but knowing Maggie, not for long.

The doorbell chimed again, and a well-dressed woman wearing a pink hat and a little too much makeup entered the store. She wrinkled her nose as if she smelled something bad, then refocused her attention on Anna. "Hello, I'm Clarissa," she said with a shrill voice and her hand held out. "My husband is the mayor of Magnolia Hill, and I'm the chair of community affairs at the Magnolia Hill Chamber of Commerce. You must be Anna Weaver, Maggie's daughter."

"I am." Anna stepped forward and accepted her handshake. Immediately, she wanted to recoil when she smelled the woman's pungent, flowery perfume but kept her composure. She wasn't sure what to think of this woman, but warning bells sounded in her head. "It's very nice to meet you, Clarissa," she said. "Thank you for stopping by. Can I help you find something?"

Clarissa inspected her, then looked around the store. "I saw the flyers for the new class tonight and wanted to see what all the buzz was about with the remodel. I also wanted to let Maggie know that I hadn't seen her at the Chamber meetings for years. All local business owners attend our monthly meetings and events, except for your mother. Maybe you will attend Thursday's noon meeting at the Chamber?"

Anna cringed. "I'll do my best, you know, with the remodeling and such."

"I see." Clarissa looked down at Anna's paint-spotted shorts and T-shirt as if to contemplate her next insult. "I like what you've done to this shop. It looks welcoming."

Anna was about to thank Clarissa for the unexpected compliment, when the woman continued to speak.

"But you need to do something about this old house smell in here. Do you have a mold problem? I know someone in town who can fix that."

"Thank you, Clarissa, we'll take that into consideration." This woman was just full of joy and obviously not interested in buying yarn. "Please do let me know if I can help you find something in the store."

Clarissa took the hint. "Oh, that's okay, my dear. I have to get back to the office. Remember, Thursday at noon at the Chamber. I expect you both to be there." With that, Clarissa turned and let herself out.

Anna exhaled. She knew she'd encounter one of the upper-class townsfolk sooner or later. Although, the more she thought about it, Clarissa had a point. The store had a slightly musky smell she needed to address. Maybe they could add fragrance candle- or soap-making classes to their schedule for the time being. She also knew that staying connected with the Chamber and other local business owners was essential for the success of a small-town shop. Why was Maggie not as engaged as she'd been before Anna left Magnolia Hill?

The doorbells chimed again, and Maggie entered the shop with Woofus dawdling in behind her. "Did I just see Clarissa Harrington leave the store?"

Anna rolled her eyes and took a deep breath. "Yes."

"What did the witch want?"

"I see you're on good terms with her,"

Anna said, sarcasm dripping like maple syrup.

"Not at all."

"She invited us to the next Chamber meeting in no uncertain terms and said the place reeked like house rot."

"That doesn't surprise me. Besides, what did she expect? This building is over ninety years old. Of course it has a certain ambience."

"Mom, maybe we should go to this Chamber meeting since we're revamping the store and offering new programs. I think it would be a great idea to spread the word and connect with other store owners."

"I know them all."

"Mom, what's bothering you? Did something happen between you and Clarissa?"

"I just can't stand her! She is a snobby, hoity-toity know-it-all." She paused.

"Mom?"

"Okay, if you have to know, I used to be involved in local events and cross-advertised with local stores. I was in the running for director of the Chamber, when she became flirty with the mayor and turned all the other business owners against me. That woman is evil!"

"I see." Anna glanced at the bulletin board by the door. "I'm glad you kept a good relationship with some local store owners."

"Those are the ones that didn't turn on me, and I support them the best I can."

She gave Maggie a hug. "Mom, you have a heart of gold. So, how about you come with me tomorrow? I bet there are people who would love to see you."

"Or not."

"Mom, if you want this shop to be the cozy hangout it once was, you have to make peace with the locals. There's no way around it. People talk, I get it, but a little bit of sugar…"

"No!"

She'd have to work harder. Anna gave her a pleading look that always worked on her mom.

Maggie caved. "Okay, I'll come, but I'll make no promises it'll turn out well."

* * *

Last night's class was a success, and even more customers visited the shop today. Anna was exhausted, and

Maggie didn't look any better when six o'clock came around.

"We're closing the shop on time today," Maggie ordered.

"But, Grandma!" Ashleigh protested. "We need to..."

"Nope. Whatever it is, it can wait," she said, leaving no room to argue. "We will go home, order a pizza, and do nothing for the rest of the evening."

"Yes, ma'am!" Anna saluted her, then grabbed her purse and car keys. "Doing nothing it is."

Doing nothing, however, left Anna antsy. Maggie kept the TV turned on the news with Jason covering a vicious front moving through Georgia, which already prompted warnings to the west of them. She knew her mother did it on purpose.

"It could get dicey for the folks in the counties highlighted in yellow," Jason said, pointing at the map. "Please remember to keep your weather radio turned on and a flashlight near your bed before you go to sleep."

His voice faded away as sadness filled her heart. It didn't matter if she still loved him. He wasn't ready for a relationship either, and he had told her so. If it was meant to be, she could wait. It was for the best.

Before she could let herself fall deeper into despair, she walked over to the dining room table and opened her laptop. She had to distract herself, and she knew exactly how she could prove herself worthy to the community tomorrow.

Anna scoured the internet for craft related treats that she could take to the meeting to win over the hearts of local business owners, since she was the new girl in town and Maggie had been missing in action from anything chamber related for a while.

It only took her five minutes on Pinterest to find the perfect dessert. "I can do that," she whispered and clicked on the recipe for yarn ball cookies. She unplugged her laptop and carried it to the kitchen. The pantry was full of baking supplies, and none of the ingredients she needed looked unusual. Even the instructions were simple enough to follow at first glance.

"What are you doing, sweet pea?" Maggie asked.

"I'm baking cookies for the meeting tomorrow."

"Uh-oh," Maggie held up her hands. "Lord help her!"

"Mom, I got this," she said, with a wooden spoon in one hand.

Maggie grabbed her tea and walked to the living room. "Well, call me if you need me. I'll watch Jason covering the storm."

"I won't need you, Mom."

 She pulled a large bowl out of the cabinet and mixed the flour, sugar, eggs, and butter to make the cookie dough. She couldn't find the parchment paper, but figured that aluminum foil would do the trick. Anna shoved the baking sheet with the cookies in the oven, then realized that she had forgotten to preheat it. *Oh well,* she thought, *I'll just let them go a few minutes longer.*

While the cookies were baking, she made the icing and divided it up into four small bowls to make blue, red, green, and yellow yarn colors to decorate the cookies with. The idea was to squirt the icing over each cookie in thin strings to make them look like balls of yarn. Happy with her icing colors, she stood back and admired her work. Only one thing was missing—the cookies.

"The cookies!" she yelled as panic set in. When she opened the oven door, a gray plume of smoke greeted her with the sharp bite of burned cookies. She grabbed an oven mitt, pulled out the baking sheet, and sat it on the stove. Her perfect cookies now resembled flat brownish-black briquettes. "The timer…"

"What's that smell? Is something burning?" Ashleigh called from upstairs.

"Don't worry, baby girl!" Maggie said. "Your mom said she got it!"

"Okay!" Ashleigh's door closed again.

Deflated, like her cookies, she turned on the overhead vent to suck up the smoke. The last thing she needed was the fire department show up on their doorstep because of her Pinterest fail. She should've known better, even though the instructions seemed so easy. When would she learn that baking was not something she should attempt unsupervised?

Anna grabbed the cookie sheet and opened the trash can. The cookies stuck to the aluminum foil like superglue. Why she even tried to pull them off was beyond her, because none of the treats were edible anymore. She tore the foil from the edges of the cookie sheet and tossed the burnt mess into the garbage. The slamming sound of the lid just added insult to her wounded soul.

She sat the cookie sheet on the counter, then stared at the small bowls of icing. Maybe she could salvage it and decorate a pack of store-bought sugar cookies in the morning—or she could simply eat it straight, like she used to when decorating Ashleigh's birthday cakes, before she resorted to buy them from the bakery at the grocery store. Anna picked up a teaspoon from the counter. Just a little taste… She smiled in anticipation of impending bliss.

Anna dipped her spoon into the frosting then licked it clean with one swoop. However, as the rich, sweet frosting melted in her mouth, her face contorted and her body shivered as if a rabbit had crossed her grave.

Not ready to accept total defeat and determined to show up with something in hand at tomorrow's chamber meeting, she typed "craft-related gifts" in the Pinterest search field for a quick non-food project.

"Bingo," she said as she saw a picture of tiny crochet balls made from leftover yarn. She could fill small satchels with small Spinning Yarns tags on them and hand them out at the meeting tomorrow.

"I'm sorry your cookies didn't turn out," Maggie said as she walked into the kitchen to refill her tea.

"That's okay, Mom. I found something better." She showed Maggie the picture. "Do you want to help me with these gifts?"

"Sure, I have a bunch of leftover yarn in the craft room closet. I think there's also a pack of satchels we didn't use for Mary Miller's daughter's wedding. Let me go get them."

Two hours later, and on a mission, they sat on the couch together crocheting away and filling the small satchels on the coffee table with the miniature crocheted balls of yarn in record time. She had to admit, they were adorable.

"I missed our craft evenings," Maggie said. "I'm so happy you moved back home."

"Me, too, Mom," Anna said. "I carried on the tradition with Ash when she was younger. We looked for fun knitting patterns and made movie-themed scarves and hats to wear during the winter."

"You no longer do crafts together?"

Anna shook her head. "When she became a teenager, she lost interest in hanging out with me. I guess knitting and crocheting with your mom is not a cool thing to brag about in school when you're in middle and high school."

"That's too bad," Maggie said. "Anna, something is still off. Do you want to tell me what happened last weekend?"

Anna shrugged. "It was wet and windy."

Maggie dropped her hands with her crochet needle and yarn wrapped around her finger onto her lap and gave her a you-know-what-I-mean look. "That, you told me already."

Anna took the hint. *Might as well,* she thought. She knew better than trying to gloss things over with her mom, so she gave in and spilled the beans. "Okay, we got along well in the excitement of the storm, and we kissed, but we decided we'd better not date right now."

"Why the heck not? What possible reason could be so important not to go for it?"

"Mom! I just got divorced from an abusive husband. I have to get my life together. There's no room for a relationship. Besides, I don't think he's ready, either, you know, with his wife gone."

"Oh, excuses, excuses!" she said, clicking her tongue.

"That's what Jenna said."

"Jason and you were inseparable back then. I saw how you looked at each other when he picked you up this weekend."

Anna sighed. "I want to talk to him, but what if he isn't ready? He said so on the way home. I mean, how can I compete with the memories of his wife?"

"Oh, sweetheart," she said, and drew her into a tight embrace and rubbed her back. "You won't have to compete. You already made your own memories together long before then."

"He's still grieving."

Maggie released her from her embrace and put her hand on hers. "Listen to me, Anna," she said, her grip now firm. "He has always been your friend. Start there. He needs someone in his life, even Sarah says so. He's miserable." Maggie squeezed her hand one more time for good measure then let go. "I know how it feels, because I lost your dad early, too. When you first saw Jason at the park, both of your faces brightened. I knew right then and there you two were meant for each other, yet, both of you keep telling yourselves why you weren't." She shook her head. "It's a mystery to me!"

"What if I don't deserve someone like Jason? What if I'm not good enough for him?" Anna looked down at her body and sucked in her belly to hide the extra roll of skin that showed through her blouse. When she no longer could hold her breath, she let her belly go again and hung her head.

"Anna, listen to yourself. Do you really believe Jason cares about a few extra pounds? He loves you. And don't ever, never ever, think you are not worthy of love! There are still good men in this world, and Jason's one of them."

Her anger subsided and warmth radiated when Maggie stroked her cheek. "Sweetie, you're my everything and perfect in any way."

Anna's frown lifted. "You're my mom. You're supposed to say that."

Maybe, just maybe, her mom was right. Looking back at the Tybee trip, they were happy together, at least for the first half of the weekend, and the girls were getting along great. What if there was hope? What if she would entertain the thought she was worthy of good things happening in her life—namely Jason?

She could feel Maggie's eyes burn a hole into her head. *Seriously,* she thought. *What could be the worst that could happen?* Yes, she still had to deal with the trauma of her marriage to Luke, but who was to say that she couldn't be happy and heal at the same time. Jason was also the kind of guy who'd support her through her recovery, whatever it took, may it be therapy sessions or weekly group meetings. Anna finally realized that healing and happiness did not have to be mutually exclusive. And if it was true that he was as miserable as she was, it was rather silly to wait on each other to make the first move. "Okay. I'll talk to him. But first I'll get some sleep." She kissed her mom on the forehead. "Good night."

Upstairs in her room, Anna could still hear Jason's voice blaring through the house. Sound did travel with these wooden floors. "And now back to you, Anna," he said. "Oh, forgive me. Yvonne."

Anna held back a laugh. Had he just called the female news anchor by the wrong name? If that wasn't a sign... She dug out her old journal and took yet another trip down memory lane. Within minutes, she drifted off to sleep to the rumble of thunder and her journal between her face and her pillow. If only her dreams could come true.

Chapter 19

When she woke in the morning, Anna had to peel a page off her cheek—the page she had written about Jason taking her to their secret spot at the creek, where they had spent countless hours talking, fishing, and kissing. She sighed, then made herself get out of bed. She had a busy day ahead of her.

Anna was looking forward to today's Chamber meeting and getting to meet a few of the other shop owners in town. What she wasn't looking forward to was running into Clarissa again. The woman was just overbearing. Anna wasn't sure she was ready to endure another barrage of subtle insults wrapped up in a box with a pretty bow on top and delivered with a sweet-as-sugar poisonous smile. Maybe, by some miracle, the woman would miss today's meeting. But she didn't hold her breath for that to happen.

Looking at the yarn ball satchels they made last night, she felt a sense of pride and joy. At last, she had picked a project she was good at. She lined a small basket with pink gift paper and neatly arranged the yarn satchels to take to the meeting. As a finishing touch, she attached a label with their business name and phone number to the satchel strings.

That was it. This was the missing link in making Spinning Yarns a success.

She had to spark this feeling, one of accomplishment and pride, in her mom's customers. Maybe they could offer classes for making small and simple gifts for a variety of occasions. There certainly was no shortage of ideas online. The sky was the limit.

Maggie and Anna arrived at the Chamber about fifteen minutes before the meeting started. She already recognized a few faces. Sean was talking to Clarissa when he spotted her.

Immediately, he excused himself and strolled over to greet them. "Hey, Anna. It's so good to see you," he said. "Thank you for rescuing me from the clutches of Clarissa Harrington." He held his hand to his heart. "What would I have done if you hadn't shown up for this meeting to save me?"

"You're very welcome," she said. "What brings you here?"

Sean nodded his head toward Clarissa. "The mayor's wife asked me to give a talk about property theft and what business owners can do to prevent it."

"Do we have a lot of issues with theft and other crime against businesses in Magnolia Hill?"

"Not so much in this town. We had a few instances lately with teenagers pranking stores on the weekends, but nothing too serious. It just doesn't hurt to be aware."

Maggie rested a hand on Anna's shoulder. "Since you two found each other, I'll head on over to say hello to Lena Miller. She took over the ice cream parlor after her grandpa died. I'm sure you remember Mr. Miller?"

Anna had fond memories of buying ice cream on sweltering hot summer days. Jason took her almost every weekend when they were dating. Chocolate chip cookie dough on a fresh waffle cone with chocolate sprinkles was her favorite then, and still was today. She made a mental note to take the girls out for a treat one day while it was still warm. "I do remember Mr. Miller. How could I forget him? He always gave me extra chocolate sprinkles on my ice cream," she said with a smile. "Go on and visit —I bet you have a lot to catch up on."

"Watch out," Maggie said, pointing toward the far end of the parking lot as she walked away. "That's Miriam Sue Webster heading your way. With you being the new girl in town, I'd say stay clear of her unless you want to be on the front page of the Magnolia Hill

Times again." Maggie winked at her and walked away.

Sean took her by the arm and steered her to the side of the building. "That should keep her away for a minute," he said with a satisfied grin on his face.

"I wouldn't be so sure," Anna said. "She probably thinks she'll find a juicy story with us hiding behind the building."

He waved her off. "Just let me do the talking if she pops around the corner."

Once they were out of sight and out of range from prying eyes and ears, he became more somber. "Hey, look, Anna," he started. "I'm not sure what's going on between you and Jason, and it may not be my business, but he's been acting strange since the hurricane weekend. He's not himself, if you know what I mean."

Not him, too, Anna thought. She had no idea that her relationship with Jason, or lack thereof, would affect this many people, but Anna had to remind herself that she was in a small town again, not in Colorado Springs where you barely knew your neighbor. "I know. We have some things to work out. Sean, you've always been my friend, and you're close to Jason. I don't know." She paused. "But do you think he's ready to date? I mean, really ready?"

"If you're asking me if you two should take the plunge, then I would say, Yes, yes, yes! What are you waiting for? You need each other."

"But what about his wife?"

"I knew Caroline. She was kind, gentle, and caring. She would want him to be happy, but Jason is honest and loyal, almost to his own detriment. Since you've returned, he hasn't stopped talking about you." Sean put his arm around her shoulder for a friendly squeeze. "Talk to each other."

This, coming from their best friend, gave Anna even more hope and the courage she desperately needed. Not that Jenna's and her mom's opinion didn't count. There were no storms on the forecast tonight, so she was determined to call him after dinner. "I will." The thought of a possible rejection terrified her.

"All right, everybody," Clarissa's voice screeched across the parking lot. "We're starting the meeting in about two minutes. Please come inside and take your seats."

Anna was about to walk through the Chamber doors when she heard a familiar voice call her name from behind. It was Jenna hurrying toward her.

Anna waited for her to catch up. "Hi."

"Hey," Jenna said, out of breath.

She sensed that something was off. "Uh-oh. I don't like that look. What's up?"

"Come on in, everybody, don't be shy and no lollygaggin'." Clarissa's shrill voice carried over the chatter. "We have a full agenda today."

Jenna rolled her eyes. "I can't stand that woman. I'll tell you after the meeting."

Whatever it was, it seemed important, but it would have to wait. Anna set the basket with the satchels of crocheted balls of yarn on the middle of the large conference table and took the seat between Maggie and Sean. The pungent smell of Clarissa's perfume overwhelmed her senses. Never did she think that woman's fragrance could be worse than it was the other day. She was wrong. Her nose started itching, and it took all of her self-control not to sneeze. She picked up the agenda from the table and glanced at the list of speakers. She was about halfway through the list when the door to the conference room open and a flushed Jason entered the room. He still wore a Band-Aid on his forehead that stuck out like a sore thumb. At least it was tan, and not bright white like the one she had slapped on his forehead a few days ago.

"Sorry I'm late, everybody. Don't mind me," he said as he squeezed between the chairs and the wall to get to a vacant seat.

What was he doing here? Her heart raced ninety miles a minute, and for some reason, she became a little light-headed. He stopped right behind her, bent down, and whispered in her ear. "Let's talk when the meeting is over," he said, then continued his way to the empty chair at the end of the table and sat down. As soon as he was settled, he lifted his head and their gazes met.

Anna's heart raced, and she felt a bit woozy. It must be the heat, she tried to justify her reaction to him in her head, and reached for her bottle of water.

Clarissa cleared her throat and began to speak again, successfully ruining the moment. "Thank you all for joining us for today's meeting. Please welcome back Maggie Weaver, the owner of Spinning Yarns, and her daughter, Anna, who just moved back into town. Together, they've been rejuvenating the shop and are now also expanding their class offerings tailored to all ages. Please pay them a visit to see how the shop has improved." Most of the members clapped.

Miriam Sue Webster, the reporter, stared at Anna. Great, eventually they'd have to talk to her. If they played their cards right, the Spinning Yarns shop could be on the front page to announce the grand opening. She made a note to pursue that idea in a few weeks when they would be ready for an open house.

"Back to the agenda, we have two presentations today following the business portion of this gathering..."

Anna was distracted the entire meeting and only caught bits and pieces of the announcements. All she could think about was Jason who was sitting so close to her, yet so far away. She wasn't sure how their conversation after the meeting would go. Her planned phone conversation tonight was moved up to a face-to-face in less than an hour. Anna's hands went numb and her palms sweaty. She would have to call Jenna later to find out what she needed to tell her. Jason came first.

She stole a look past the other members and caught Jason staring at her before he looked away.

He seemed nervous and fiddled with the corner of his agenda, but then raised his head and smiled at her, his face slightly blushing.

Her heart fluttered, and the dizziness returned. She wanted to look away but couldn't pry herself away from his longing eyes.

"Mr. Morrison, it is your turn…"

Clarissa urged and waited for his response.

Torn out of her spell, she noticed that all eyes were on Jason. The reddish hue on his face deepened.

"Of course," he said, flustered. He rubbed his hands on his pant legs, then stood up to deliver his talk about how to save energy as the weather changed in the next few weeks.

Something odd was going on, though. She noticed that several members checked their cell phones and began to whisper, followed by uncomfortable stares aimed at Maggie. Someone was showing her phone to Miriam Sue, who nodded and stared at Anna. What was happening?

* * *

After the meeting, Anna exited the building. Some of the members were still pointing and whispering. Her original intent to mingle and meet other shop owners evaporated with all this hush-hush secrecy around her. She needed air. Besides, Jason wanted to talk to her, and the meeting room was not the place for a private conversation.

She watched him make his way toward her, when he suddenly stopped. He pulled his phone out of his pocket, and his expression changed into a frown.

Her hopes evaporated faster than condensation from her cup dripping onto the paved parking lot.

"Ah, Anna, I'm sorry. I have a minor emergency at work," he said, raking his hand through his hair. "I'll try to come see you if I can break away from the TV station before my next broadcast. We need to talk about this in person. I'm sorry about having to run."

"Yes, of course," she said. "I wanted to talk to you, too." That was the story of her life. Something good was about to happen, at least that's what she hoped for, and within seconds it was taken away from her. Again.

He waved at her one more time and off he went.

Anna hung her head, but there was nothing she could do about it now. A few of the meeting attendees caught up with her, thanking her for coming. "Those little baggies you brought are just adorable," a woman in a blue travel agency polo said. "Are you teaching classes at your shop?"

Her heart skipped a beat. Anna's gift bags turned out to be quite a conversation starter before the whispers began. "Yes, we are developing a new class schedule as we speak. We already offer bracelet classes for teens. In the next few weeks, we hope to add gift-making workshops and traditional knitting and crocheting courses with a fresh twist."

"Oh, I'm so excited! I love crafts! That'll give me something to do in the evenings." The woman let out a sigh. "Sometimes I wish I was married like all of my friends. At least they have someone to keep them company. I'm the last one who didn't tie the knot yet." She cleared her throat. "I'm sorry, sometimes I tend to overshare." She reached out her hand. "My name is Mandy, by the way. I own the Happy Waves Travel Agency down the road."

"That's okay, Mandy. Sometimes marriage isn't all that it's cracked up to be. I'm Anna."

"Oh? Maybe we just haven't met the right one yet." Mandy's lips turned up into a smile. "I saw you and Jason on the news during the hurricane. And today in the meeting…"

Anna's face flushed.

"I am so sorry! I overstepped again. Let's start over. Hi, I'm Mandy, and I'd love to attend some of your gift-making classes."

They both laughed. "You know, you remind me of one of my bubbly paramedic friends in Colorado. She was a hoot!"

"Well, thank you!"

"Anyway, if you're interested in learning something in particular, we'll try to make it happen. You can come by the shop anytime or leave a request via the contact page on our website. All our social media info is also printed on the back side of the label." She pointed at the satchel Mandy held in her hand.

"Oh, that's wonderful! I might just swing by the shop on my lunch break one day to find out what's new." She checked her watch. "Oh my gosh, I've gotta run. It was so good to meet you, Anna, and I'll see you soon," Mandy said, sliding her sunglasses down from the top of her head and then rushing down the street.

It took all the effort she could muster to stay calm. Now if they could get a handful of young mothers excited about the shop and their classes too, word-of-mouth would do the rest. Spinning Yarns could once again be the popular community hangout it had been when she was young.

She walked toward Maggie and two of the other shop owners who had gathered in the parking lot to mingle. She was about to join them when Jenna called her name from behind.

Anna almost had forgotten about her friend in the excitement. She turned around. "Hey, what's going on?"

"Listen, I will give it to you straight. There's a rumor going around town about your dad."

"My dad?"

"Grace is telling everyone that your grandfather paid off your dad to leave town, you know, with him being from Puerto Rico."

"What? Grandpa would have never done that!" Anna said. "That can't be true."

"I wish I could tell you more, but that's all I've heard. I just wanted to give you a heads-up."

"Thanks, Jenna. No wonder people in the meeting were giving us these strange looks, especially the reporter—what's her name? Miriam Sue?"

"Yes, Miriam Sue Webster. Be careful. She can be your best friend or your worst enemy, depending on where you stand with her."

"I'll keep that in mind," Anna said. "I think I'll have a talk with my mom."

Anna's mind had been going a hundred miles a minute on the ride back to the shop. That didn't even make sense. Her grandfather had been a kind man. No way did he bribe her dad to jet for the money and an easy way out.

A few minutes later, Maggie and Anna arrived at the shop, and Maggie poured them each a glass of iced tea.

"What's bothering you, honey?" Maggie asked. "You've been quiet since the meeting let out. If it was those hoity-toity witches being rude at the meeting, ignore them. They always have something to gossip about."

 "Mom, why did Dad leave?"

Maggie looked taken aback. "I don't know, sweetie. You know all that I know. Why?"

"Grace is spreading a rumor that Grandpa paid him off to leave. Is that true?"

"Anna, I don't know. One day he was here and telling me he'll love me forever, and the next day he was gone. Just like that, without a warning. Neither Grandpa nor Grandma told me anything before they passed. Do you think..." Maggie's eyes filled with tears.

Chapter 20

Ashleigh slammed the door shut behind her and threw her backpack on the floor. Never had she been this humiliated in her whole life. She wanted to scream. "Mom!"

Her mom came out of the kitchen to meet her halfway. "Wow, Ashleigh. A little less violence will go a long way. What's going on?"

"It's all over school. 'The new girl's grandpa loves money more than his daughter.' Being that I'm the new girl, and my grandpa split, guess who they're talking about? What happened? Did he really leave us for a big check?" The words just kept coming. "Have you and Grandma lied to me this whole time?"

"No, honey. I would never lie to you." Her mom pulled out a chair for her. "Sit and tell me from the beginning what happened at school today and who was behind it."

Ashleigh plopped onto the chair, not caring if Sarah would have said it looked unladylike. "We were at lunch when these Lakeview Heights girls were talking and pointing at me and texting on their phones. I got up from my table and confronted them." Just the thought alone made her tighten her fists and her heart race. "They said that Grandpa ran back to Mexico, or wherever he was from, and spent the money in less than a month, having himself a good time."

Her mom dropped her head into her propped-up hands on the table, then said, "I'm so sorry this happened to you. I don't know what to tell you about your grandpa or if the rumor is even true."

"It's embarrassing," Ashleigh said. "Grady and Sarah told me to just ignore everyone and it'll go away if it's not fun for them to talk about anymore. But, Mom, they are talking about my family."

"Yeah, high school in the country can be a different kind of cruel, but I think your friends are right."

"But now the whole town is talking about us, and school is horrible." She didn't want to go back to class tomorrow and face the taunting again.

And her bracelet classes? That dream lasted not even a week.

"Remember, sweetie, your friends will always be on your side. Grandma and I will sort this out, okay? And your bracelets will still sell."

"I wish I was back in Colorado. This never would've happened at my old school. I hate this town!"

Her mom laid a hand on her shoulder. "Sweetie, wherever you go, things can go wrong, and more often than not, life's not fair. It's what you make out of these situations that makes you strong."

"That's easy for you to say." Obviously her mom had no clue. "You ran from Colorado and dragged me with you. I would have been back in school with my friends. I'd be living with Dad. He never hurt me, only you! You took everything from me!" she yelled.

"That's not fair, Ash!" her mom said and dropped her hand from her shoulder.

Even though she was angry at the world for being stuck in the country and being ridiculed in school, watching her mom's face turn red and her eyes fill with tears made her cringe with remorse. It was too late. The words were already out.

"I had to make a decision that was the best for both of us." Her mom wiped her eyes. "Colorado Springs was too expensive for us to live on my income alone. And, to be honest, I'm kinda scared of your dad now." Her mom took a deep breath. "Coming here was the best option we had. I needed to be home and around friends and family, and Grandma needs us, too." She smiled. "Look who is sticking with you. You have Sarah and Grady. Friendships here are for life."

"I know, and I'm sorry, Mom. I just miss home."

"My hope for you is that in time you'll give this town and the people in it a chance."

Ashleigh could feel her anger fade away. Deep down inside, she knew that her mom was right. She really enjoyed helping with the shop, the classes, and the website. It gave her purpose along with a little extra money to spend with Sarah and Grady at the ice cream shop. Thinking of it that way, those Lakeview Heights girls held a lot less power, if any, over her.

"Speaking of Grady," her mom continued. "How are things going? A little birdie told me you two are dating?"

Ashleigh's face heated, then she smiled. "We have a date tomorrow evening after practicing one last time for Saturday's skating competition."

"Oh? Are you ready?"

"What for, the date or the competition?"

Her mom grinned. "For both. Do we need to have a talk?"

She rolled her eyes. Please, spare me... "No, Mom. We've had that talk a million times. We're just going to Mamaw's and having an ice cream at Miller's afterward. It'll be totally innocent." She flashed her a smile.

"Well, I'm not 100 percent sure about that totally innocent part, but I trust your judgment. I also hope you trust me enough to come talk to me about anything—boyfriend related or not."

Ashleigh got up from the chair, grabbed her backpack, and headed for the stairs. "I do, Mom. I'm going to my room to do my homework." She stopped with one foot on the steps and turned back to her mom. "Maybe you and Grandma can find out more about Grandpa. I wonder if he's still alive."

Anna had had enough. She didn't care if Grace wanted to attack her, but she wouldn't let her get away with dragging her family into this mess. Grace was playing dirty and today it would stop for good! While Ash was upstairs doing her homework, she grabbed her car keys off the kitchen counter and let the screen door slam behind her.

She drove across town toward Grace's old family home on Gardenia Street, determined to fight for her family. She assumed Grace still lived in that same old run-down house she had lived in back then. As a young girl, Anna had always taken the long way to the ice cream parlor to avoid confrontations with her bully. This time, she sought it. She was past scared. Adrenaline made her hands shake and her heart pump hard as she'd only experienced once before less than a year ago. Of course, she hit every red light in town, which meant two of them. Her fingers tapped the steering wheel as she waited for the light to turn green.

Pulling up at Grace's driveway, she noticed much of the once white paint had chipped from the wooden siding of the small house. Anna wasn't surprised. A what used-to-be green Ford Taurus but was now a rusted heap of dented metal sat under a corroded car port. Nothing had changed except for the car.

With dread, she turned off her car engine. *Remember why you are here*, she told herself. With Maggie and Ashleigh's still images in her mind, she took one deep breath of courage. "It's now or never."

Before she could change her mind, she slammed her car door shut and climbed up the rickety wooden steps onto Grace's rotten and moss-covered porch. The yard was overgrown with weeds, and the trash can was full and reeking to high heavens. She shriveled her nose. Trash pickup wasn't until the end of the week.

With her heart pounding in her chest, she raised her hand and knocked on the door. Deep inside, she hoped that nobody was home, but she knew that if she'd have to confront her a second time, she might not have the guts.

She heard footsteps approaching on the other side of the door. Her body tensed, and for a second, she felt the urge to run.

Grace opened the door with a sneer on her face. A pair of oversize sunglasses covered her eyes. Her tank top partially covered a fresh bruise on her shoulder.

Anna could smell the alcohol on her and almost felt sorry for Grace. Almost.

"Lookie here what the cat dragged in," Grace said with mock joy. In an instant, her facade morphed into an evil smirk. "What do you want, Fatty Annie?" she said with disgust.

"You know why I'm here, Grace." She

put her hands on her hips. "Who told you about my dad?"

Grace laughed. "I'm not going to tell you," she slurred, then paused as if to contemplate what to say next. "Well, okay, it's none of your business, but if you need to know, my boyfriend's uncle worked at your grandparent's mansion as a gardener. Must be nice to have a rich family."

Her evil laugh chilled Anna to the bone.

"Oh, never mind! He lost that property in some bad real-estate investments a few years later. Humbled him down a good bit. Your grandma had to open that pitiful shop downtown to make a living, but you knew that already," Grace added to drive home the point.

Anna's blood was boiling, but she had to stay calm. She needed to hear what happened to her father, at least one version of it. "So what did your boyfriend's uncle say?"

"Suddenly you're paying attention, aren't you?" she slurred as she steadied herself by leaning against the door frame. When Anna didn't bat an eye, Grace continued. "Housekeeping staff said that they saw a check made out for ten thousand dollars to your dad in his office. He also remembered your mother crying like a baby for weeks after he went missing." Grace made a pouty face. "So sad."

"Who's at the door?" a moody male voice called out from the back of the house.

"Nobody important," Grace yelled back.

"Then shut the door! You're letting all the flies and hot air in."

"Hold on a minute, Moose!"

A brown bottle flew toward them and shattered on the wall, nearly missing Grace's head. "Close the door!" Moose hollered again.

Anna jumped back. To her surprise, her anger evaporated and was replaced with compassion for the woman standing in front of her. "Grace, this guy is dangerous. I see your bruises. Please don't make the same mistake I did. I got away. You may not be so lucky."

Grace's facial expression softened for a moment, then turned to stone again. "What I do is none of your business. We're done here," she yelled and slammed the door in Anna's face.

Anna beat on the door with her fists. "Please, Grace, trust me on this."

"Go away!" she called out from behind the door.

Anna opened her fists and laid her hands against the door. With a calm voice she said, "Grace, you've got to believe me."

There was nothing left to say, so she turned away and walked back to her car. She should've felt good about standing up to Grace, but instead, she felt pity. The last thing she wanted was Grace's picture splattered across the front page of the Magnolia Hill Times. She paused and looked back at the house one more time before getting into her car. Grace was standing behind the thin curtain, watching her. With a sense of doom, Anna turned the key in the ignition. "Grace, I tried," she whispered, then drove off.

Chapter 21

Jason paced in his kitchen. It was Saturday, the day of Grady and Ashleigh's skateboarding competition. The town had been abuzz when he went for a quick run earlier that morning to shake off his nervous energy. It didn't help, and there was only one person to blame for his unsettled state—Anna.

Every time Jason had built up the courage to see her over the last few days, it had left him just as fast. What was wrong with him? He never had problems talking to people. For crying out loud, he was a public figure broadcasting on TV almost every day and enjoyed making appearances at local events to support the community. Yet today, his nerves had the better of him. Anna would be at the skate park watching Ash and Grady compete.

"Hey, Dad," Sarah said as she came down the stairs. "Are you ready?"

"Yes, I am. Let me just get my..." He patted his jeans pockets, then looked around the kitchen. "Have you seen my keys?"

Sarah laughed. "Dad, they are on top of the washer. Will you stop pacing already?" she asked. "You are acting like a senior waiting to ask a girl to prom."

Was it that obvious? "I'm just a little scatterbrained this morning. I need more coffee."

"Nope. I think it's Anna," she said, teasing him. "You know she'll be there."

The girls had been relentless in playing matchmaker all week long. "My Mom and Grandma watch you on TV every evening," Ashleigh had said.

"And you seem much happier when we talk about Ashleigh's mom," Sarah had added.

"Go make more bracelets," he'd kept telling them, but they'd only giggled in return. The last thing he needed was constant reminders of how miserable he was without her.

Jason poured another cup of coffee. His mind drifting off once again to the last time he'd seen Anna at the

Chamber meeting on Wednesday. He'd never forget that longing look when they made eye contact. He'd known he had to talk to her. Her smile had made his insides turn into mush. Had he been crazy or had her eyes sparkled when she saw him walk in? His logical mind had taken a permanent leave of absence that very moment, and he hadn't been the same since. Dang his national station manager for dropping in for a surprise visit.

"Dad!" Sarah yelled.

"What?" Jason looked down at his into his giant Best Dad Ever mug. Coffee had spilled all over the counter. He sat the coffee pot down. "Quick, give me something to clean up this mess!"

She handed him two dish towels. "Uh, your cup is empty."

"Thanks, Sherlock," he said and mopped up the hot brew.

"I think you need to see someone about this. I'm beginning to worry about you."

"Oh yeah?"

"Yeah," Sarah said. "My friend's mom is a paramedic, you know."

He gave her a light jab into her shoulder. "Does she know much about the heart?"

Sarah nodded. "Loads!"

"All right then. Let's go see her!" he said and grabbed the bouquet of flowers he had picked early that morning from his garden. It was held together with a post office rubber band— not the prettiest way to hold them together, but Sarah refused to give up one of her hair scrunchies, when she told him they didn't have any ribbons in the house. The dingy rubber band would have to do.

They walked out to the driveway.

"Wait, Dad. I forgot something," Sarah said.

"Be quick about it," Jason said. "I'm on a mission…"

Sarah ran into the house and a few moments later emerged with a red Colorado ballcap on her head.

Jason tilted his head to his side. "You're wearing a ballcap?"

"Uh, yes. Ashleigh gave it to me. She has a bunch more. It'll be great to keep the sun out of my eyes at the skate park today."

He smiled. "I know what it does, but you never liked to wear them before. You always said they mess up your hair, and they don't go with nice clothes."

"Well, I changed my mind," she said. "This one fits me just right, and I like it. It keeps my bangs out of my face, too."

He shook his head. He'd been trying to tell her all these years, but she took after her mom, who was not much into wearing hats. Instead, Caroline wore her hair up in classy updos and accented the look with a nice pair of sunglasses.

Still holding the flowers, he remembered that they were in a hurry. "Alright, then, let's get going," he said to get his daughter moving.

Jason almost smashed his fingers when he slammed the driver's side door of his truck shut. A complication he couldn't afford. Not now. He was on a mission to win back his love, and he couldn't wait to get to her.

Everything seemed to go in favor of him trying again. He wasn't much of a risk-taker when it came to love, but Anna was worth the risk of rejection. The worst thing she could say was no, and he'd have to accept that if she did. But if he really loved her, he had to try again, and by golly, he was ready. Putting the pedal to the metal, he hoped that he didn't get pulled over on his way to the skate park. Nothing would come between them this time. Nothing!

"What do you think, Mom?" Anna pointed toward the old live oak tree close to the skate park. "That's a perfect spot to set up our chairs."

Maggie nodded. "Far away enough from the hubbub, but close enough to see the skateboarding," she said.

Anna was surprised that most of the town showed for the event. A few vendors and food trucks lined the edge of the park. The delicious smell of funnel cakes filled the air. They were her favorite carnival food, followed by corn dogs. A loud rumble of her stomach urged her to hurry up and get in line already, but she wasn't going to cave in that easy. Anna knew that once she bought a funnel cake, she'd be back for more goodies during the entire tournament. Bad enough that the humidity seemed to have shrunk her clothes, or was it the southern food she'd been indulging in? She wasn't sure how long she could resist the siren call of the fair food, but for now, she'd gather all her willpower and walk away. Maybe closer to lunch she'd allow herself to buy one of the funnel cakes to share.

Ashleigh dropped her skateboard and helped Maggie with her folding chair that had a small footrest attached.

"Thanks, baby girl. This will do," Maggie said and sat her insulated tumbler of sweet tea in the cupholder of her chair. "Oh, I forgot to mention, Anna." Maggie rummaged in her purse and pulled out a letter. "This came in the mail for you," she said. "I meant to give it to you at the shop, but gosh darn it, I must've forgotten about it. It does look official."

"Thanks, Mom!" Anna accepted the envelope from her and bent it back and forth to see if it felt like a driver's license. Nope. She glanced at the sender's address. It was from DPH, the Georgia Department of Public Health. Hoping it wouldn't be yet another notice from the licensing agency that they were still missing documents from the Colorado office, Anna opened the envelope. Her heart skipped a beat when she saw the content. "Yes!"

Anna did a happy dance and held the envelope to her chest. Finally.

Maggie looked at her, expecting an answer. "I take it it's good news?"

"Oh yes, it's very good news! It's my medic license. I can apply for jobs now." She crossed getting her license transferred off her mental to-do list. One step closer to independence.

"I'm glad things are falling into place for you now," Maggie said, getting up from her chair and drawing her into a hug. "You've been waiting for this, baby girl. I'm also forever grateful for your help with the shop."

"Hey, I'm not going anywhere, Mom. Besides, I love that place. Like you, I want to see it flourish again. We might move out of the house eventually, but Ashleigh and I are here to support you."

Anna knew she was ready to get back in the lifesaving business. With a steady paycheck, she could start looking at renting or buying her own home in town. Even though Maggie had told her more than once she didn't mind them staying with her, she didn't want to be a burden on her mom anymore. If she could only share a home with Jason someday, her world would be complete. But that remained to be seen, and she wasn't counting on anything at this time.

"I don't know what I would have done without you, Anna," Maggie said and sat down in her chair again. "Oh, Ashleigh, baby, I forgot to grab my crafts. Do you mind handing me that fabric bag with the floral print by the cooler?"

Ashleigh handed the colorful bag to her grandma. "Whatcha making?" she asked, peeking into it.

Anna watched her mother pull out a dainty white piece that was almost lace-like.

"I'm working on a doily for the shop window," Maggie said.

Anna reached over and let the folded project drape over her fingers. "It's beautiful, Mom," Anna said. "I love the little heart shapes going around the circle."

"You need to teach me that sometime, Grandma. It's really pretty," Ashleigh said as she dropped her backpack on the ground. She dug out her helmet and pads. "Maybe instead of hearts, though, you can show me a less girly pattern? Skulls, maybe?"

"Attention all competitors," a voice announced over the PA system. "If you haven't already done so, please make your way to the check-in table and retrieve your competitor bibs."

"Ashleigh!" a male voice called out from the parking lot.

Anna looked over and squinted her eyes into the sun and waved. Those darn shades didn't do a very good job to keep the glare out. "We have company," she said. "It's Grady and Sean."

"Do y'all mind if we sit with you?" Sean asked.

"Not at all, darling," Maggie said.

Sean sat his red University of Georgia folding chair down next to her orange and blue Colorado

Broncos one. Anna had to admit, Sean didn't look too bad in civilian clothes. It almost seemed odd now, seeing him out of uniform for the first time since she'd been back. He had grown up since high school, and his sense of fashion had improved tenfold. No more red T-shirts with green corduroys; at least she hoped so.

The kids greeted each other with an awkward hello.

Sean leaned closer to Anna. "At least they try to show some restraint around us grown-ups," he said, and nudged her shoulder with his. "I know someone who was their age when they were smooching around…"

"I did no such thing," Anna protested, the sudden heat in her face betraying her.

Sean mock-punched her on the arm.

"Ouch!" Anna rubbed the spot, trying to look as if in pain, but instead, she burst out laughing.

"Nothing has changed. You're still not a good faker," Sean said, the corners of his mouth turning into a mischievous grin.

"Dad, Ms. Weaver, are you both coming with us to check-in and sign the waivers?"

"Come on," Sean said to Anna. "Let's make it official."

"Make what official?"

"The kids. Official competitors. Why, what did you think?"

"Oh, nothing."

He smiled at her. "I think I know."

The kids walked ahead of them—*too close to one another*, Anna thought, but she couldn't blame Ashleigh.

Grady was a good kid, and she had to admit, he and Sarah had done a wonderful job helping her transition into her new life.

"You know, Jason said he was coming out this morning," Sean said with a sly grin.

"He's what?" Her heart jumped up to her throat, and her pulse began to race. She had been so preoccupied with the Grace incident and the news of her dad that she had put everything else on the back burner.

Anna looked down to check her clothes. With shaking hands, she smoothed out a few wrinkles on her T-shirt. Oh no, she wore her stained khaki shorts. Her flip-flops had also seen better days. She couldn't let Jason see her like this. She was a mess. Maybe she could run back to the house for a minute to change once Ash and Grady got checked in for the competition. She smoothed her hair back and tightened her ponytail.

Sean laughed. "Anna, stop fussing with your hair. You look fine."

"Ah, I don't know, Sean. I just am…"

"… beautiful as always."

She tucked a stubborn strand of hair behind her ear. "Thanks. I needed that. Do you mean it, though?"

"Of course I do, Weaver. Knowing Jason, he wouldn't even care if a skunk sprayed you. He'd probably want to help you get the smell off…"

"Sean!" she protested, and this time it was her turn to punch him on his arm.

He chuckled.

They were next in line. A volunteer handed Sean two waivers. "Are both your kids competing?"

He nodded. "Yes, but only one belongs to me. I'll take the second waiver, though," he said and handed it to Anna.

The moment they had signed the papers, the kids grabbed their bibs and took off toward a group of skateboarders hanging out by one of the ramps on the other side of a structure that looked like an empty pool.

 "And off they go…" Sean said and walked Anna back to the chairs to join Maggie. She was talking to another woman who had set up her chair next to theirs.

"Anna, you remember my friend Dottie Wilson, Jenna's mother, don't you?"

"I do. Hello, Mrs. Wilson. It's so good to see you again."

"My grandson Lucas is skating in the competition for the first time," Mrs. Wilson beamed.

"That's exciting…" Anna said.

The conversation ended on a dime when Anna heard Jason's voice behind her.

* * *

"I'll hang out with Grady and Ash," Anna heard Sarah call out.

"Hi, Anna."

Almost light-headed, she turned and saw Jason holding a bouquet of flowers. "Hi," she managed before her mind went blank.

He held the bouquet toward her. "Sorry these somewhat took a beating last weekend. For what it's worth, they are genuine hurricane flowers I cut from my yard this morning," he said, looking flushed and flustered.

She smiled. "Thank you," she said and accepted them. Her gaze went from the flowers up to his lips, stopped for a moment, and then up to his eyes. Was that sweat dripping from his forehead? It wasn't even that hot yet. *Maybe it's the humidity*, she thought, the same reason why she was having those palpitations again. She made a mental note to drink more fluids.

"I'm glad you're here," he said.

"Me, too. I mean, that you're here. Ashleigh is skateboarding. Well, I guess you knew that already..." Her mind was on overdrive. She had known Jason most of her life, but today, it felt as if they just met.

"I came to see you," he said, wiping his hands on his khaki shorts.

Anna's chest was full of anxious butterflies fluttering about. She wasn't sure how much more of this she could handle.

"Next up, we have Ashleigh Weaver from Magnolia Hill competing," the announcer's voice bellowed from the speakers.

Sean interrupted. "I know you two got some catching up to do, but Anna, you can't miss your daughter compete."

"I'll watch from here," Maggie said. "My heart can't take seeing that child doing these acrobatics on a rolling board."

"No worries. I'll record it with my phone for you," Sean said. "We can watch it on TV later."

Ashleigh stood at one end of the empty swimming pool structure.

Anna had faith in her daughter's abilities. That didn't mean that watching her drop into that large bowl and hanging in the air during jumps didn't make her white-knuckle her Broncos insulated cup. "Go Ash!" she called out. "You got this!"

Jason put a hand on her closest shoulder. "She's really good!"

"I know," she said, almost tempted to lean into him like she had at the beach. "When she puts her mind to it, she can do some amazing things."

"Like someone else I know," he finished, giving her shoulder a light squeeze.

Suddenly Ashleigh landed off-center and lost her footing on her board.

Anna held her breath. *Please don't fall.* A handful of bad scenarios of skate park accidents flashed through her mind. A trip to the ER would be disastrous for them right now. She couldn't afford enormous doctor bills while she was between jobs.

Like a pro, Ash took a few long steps down to the bottom of the bowl, picked up her board, and exited the structure on the shallow end.

Anna exhaled.

"Nice try!" someone called as the crowd clapped in encouragement.

"I really blew this one," Ash said as she and Sarah walked toward them. Her helmet strap hanging loose down the side of her face. "I almost had a perfect run, too."

"Don't worry, you did great." Anna tried to console her. "You'll do better on your next go."

"And now, Grady Oakley from

Magnolia Hill will show off his skills," the announcer said.

"He's starting off with a half-cab kickflip," Ashleigh said.

"A what?" Jason asked.

Sarah sighed. "It's when he enters the pipe flipping the board during a jump. It took him a while to learn, but he's got it down now."

Anna crossed herself. "It sounds dangerous."

"Yeah, it can hurt," Ashleigh admitted. "I can't do it. He's got a good chance of winning today, though."

"And you're not far behind." Sarah pointed at the scoreboard. "Third place. You can make that up."

"Only if the two other mess up, too."

"Here he goes!" Sarah called out. "Let's watch!"

Grady's mind was laser focused on the bowl. He took a running start and sped toward the edge.

To Anna's horror, a mockingbird swooped down and crossed Grady's path. She watched in slow motion as his board flew up in the air, and Grady went down into the abyss, followed by a scraping thud.

A scream next to her ripped her out of her frozen state.

She looked toward Sarah, who held her thigh, her face grimaced with pain. Grady's board landed only a few feet beside her after bouncing off her leg. The wheels were still spinning.

Anna's medic instinct kicked in. She rushed to Sarah. "Can you move your hands from your thigh?"

Sarah nodded. "It hurts."

"I know, sweetie." An elongated red area on her leg began to swell. "You're not bleeding. Why don't you sit on the grass? Ash can get you some ice to put on for now."

She then looked over the edge of the pipe and saw Grady laying on the ground. His ankle was deformed. She rushed to an area with easier access. Sean had already jumped into the bowl and helped his son sit up. Were the medics on standby sleeping in their truck? She pointed at a spectator. "Sir? Yes, you. Run to the ambulance over there and tell the paramedics that we have two injuries."

Grady clenched his teeth. His helmet had taken a beating.

"Does anything other than your leg hurt?" she asked. "Your head, your arm?"

He shook his head.

"Good. I'm going to check to make sure you don't have any other injuries," she said as she assessed him.

She could hear the rattle of the stretcher. One of the fire-medics jumped down into the bowl with his bag while the other one took the stretcher to the shallow end, left it there, then joined them carrying a spine-board.

"Sean," the first medic greeted him. "Ma'am."

"My name's Anna Weaver. I'm a paramedic," she said. "Sixteen-year-old male, fell during a jump. His right ankle is deformed, and he has multiple abrasions. Helmet took a beating on the way down, but pupils are equal and reactive."

"Well, Grady, let's get you out of this bowl and to the hospital," the medic said. "Because your helmet is badly beat-up, we'll put on a C-collar to stabilize your neck, just to be safe, in case you have a neck injury from the fall. Also, before we put you on the spine-board to take you to the stretcher, we'll stabilize your ankle, so this might hurt some, okay?"

Grady tried to nod, but the other medic held his head still. His jaw clinched in pain as the medic applied a splint.

The medics strapped Grady on a backboard and carried him out of the bowl to the stretcher.

"Dad, my board!"

"I'll get it," Sean replied, flustered.

The crowd cheered and clapped as the medics took Grady with his board on his lap to the ambulance.

Anna could tell that Sean was distraught. "He'll be fine," she said. "Kids his age bounce right back."

"I hope so."

By now, Jason, Sarah, and Ashleigh joined them.

"Sean, do you want to follow us in your vehicle?" one of the medics asked as he closed the ambulance door. "We'll take him to St. Joseph's."

"Yes, I'll catch up."

"Go, Sean!" Jason said. "We'll bring your stuff back to the house."

"Thanks, man."

"Ma'am?" the medic asked. "What ambulance service do you work for? I haven't seen you around here."

"Oh, I just moved back home from Colorado."

"Got your state license yet?"

"Just got it today."

"Well, why don't you drop an application with Magnolia Hill Fire. One of our paramedics just retired. We sure can use a good medic like you in our department. I'll put in a good word for ya, Anna Weaver."

Anna couldn't believe her luck. Aside from the accident, her day couldn't get any better.

"How's your leg, Sarah?" Anna asked as the ambulance drove off.

Sarah showed off her dark red, elongated goose egg on her thigh.

Anna winced. "I know that had to hurt."

"Yeah, it still does."

"I gotta go back," Ashleigh said. "I'm up next."

"I'm coming with," Sarah said, limping alongside her friend, leaving Anna and Jason alone.

Jason turned to Anna and put both hands on her shoulders. His eyes held hers. "You've done a great job with the kids today."

Her pulse raced once again. "That's what I'm trained to do."

His thumb brushed her cheek. "I've missed you so much since, you know, that day."

Anna thought she was going to melt into a puddle. "So did I." She wrinkled her forehead. "I wanted to talk to you, but I also wanted to give you space. You said you weren't ready."

He took a deep breath, then exhaled. "Well, Anna, I'm an idiot for letting my own stubborn values get in the way instead of fighting for you."

She put a finger on his lips. "Don't say that! First, I'm the one who has to apologize for sort of breaking up with you. A wise woman, make that three of them, told me in no uncertain terms that I needed to get my priorities straight. I thought I had, but then someone by the name of Maggie reminded me that we started out as friends. She also hinted that we might need each other more than we realized."

He laughed. "That's exactly what Sarah said to me. You don't think they all tried to set us up?"

Anna smiled and wrapped her arms around his neck. "To be honest, I'm glad they did."

"Me, too."

"So, friends again?"

He shook his head. "That won't do. We both know how that so-called friendzone worked for us."

The corner of her mouth turned into a seductive smile. "So what do you suggest instead?" she whispered.

"Well, I don't know, Ms. Weaver. I'd say we skip right to kissing."

"I think that would be a good starting point, Mr. Morrison."

Jason cupped the back of her head with one hand and let the other drop to her lower back. He pulled her closer until their lips met.

Anna was in heaven. Oh, how she had missed him.

Chapter 22

Anna and Jason sat at the kitchen table playing cards while the girls and Grady were hanging out in the living room watching a movie. After his surgery, his leg was healing faster than expected, and he now only wore a walking boot to get around. He still teased Ash that he could have taken home the trophy instead of her.

"Come on, Mom. Hurry," Anna said, more to herself than anyone. They played Rummy without keeping score while Maggie was talking on the phone. "She's been gone for over an hour."

Jason snuck a peek at her cards.

"Stop that!" Anna pushed him back. "Mind your own hand."

He laughed. "Relax, I didn't see your cards. I used to make you so mad when we were the kids' age."

"Yes, because you always cheated."

"And you always won. You didn't even give me a chance."

"That's how it's supposed to go," she replied and puckered up. "Come on, give the Queen of Rummy a well-deserved kiss."

"How can I resist?" he said and bent over for a slow, gentle kiss on her lips.

Ashleigh and Sarah walked in at that

same moment. "Ew, Mom!" Ashleigh said in disgust.

"Dad, do you have to do this in front of us kids?" Sarah said, equally uncomfortable.

Jason grabbed Anna's hand under the table.

She could feel her face flush. "It was just a little kiss, girls. Your dad and I love each other very much!"

"You'd have a cow if Grady and I did that in front of you," Ashleigh pointed out.

"Exactly! And I trust that you kids behave, even at the skate park." She knew darn well they've been kissing when she wasn't around. Maybe it was time for her and Ash to have another girl-talk over ice cream.

"Sure, Mom, whatever you say," Ashleigh said. "Who's Grandma talking to? She never spends that much time on the phone."

Anna shrugged her shoulders. "I know as much as you do. Maybe she's talking to Mrs. Wilson. Remember, she was the lady who sat with Grandma at the skating tournament?"

"Your friend with the cupcake shop's mom, right?"

"Yes," Anna said. "Even though, I'm not quite sure what they could possibly talk about this long after catching up at the skatepark."

Grady entered the kitchen. "Movie's over," he announced and piled another mountain of chips on his paper plate. His phone rang. "It's my dad," he said. "He's off work now, and he wants to take us to the drive-in theater for the double-feature. Can Ash and Sarah go?"

"Please, Dad!" Sarah begged.

"We can't get into too much trouble with the Sherriff chaperoning," Ashleigh added.

Anna glanced at Jason. "What do you think? A double-feature is a mighty long time at the theater."

Jason smiled. "I don't think they can stay up that long."

"Dad! Please!"

"What do you say, Anna?"

Anna frowned at him. "So you want me to be the bad person." She shook her head, truly enjoying teasing the kids. "If they think they can handle it."

The girls both nodded in unison.

"We can stay up that late," Sarah said. "I promise. And so can Ash. She's been talking to Grady sometimes until two in the morning."

Ashleigh glared at her friend, her face flushing bright red. "Thanks, Sarah. Do you not understand the concept of a secret between friends?"

Anna was having too much fun with this. She looked at Grady, who was just as mortified as Ashleigh. Her gaze then traveled to Jason, who also fought to keep a straight face.

"Mrs. Weaver?" Grady asked again.

Anna almost felt bad for teasing the kids that long. It was time to let them off the hook. "All right, girls. You can go," she finally said.

"One more thing," Jason added. "Sarah, tell Sean to drop you off here, and we'll ride home together after you get back."

"Will, do, Dad. Oh, and can we have a couple bucks for admission and some snacks?"

"You give 'em an inch, and they take a mile," Jason grumbled and pulled out a few bills. "This should be enough. Kids, I sure could use some help with painting the fence at my house tomorrow." He winked at Anna and squeezed her hand twice.

"Sure thing," Grady said and took Ashleigh's hand. "Let's wait for my dad outside."

Anna liked how Jason handled the kids and thoroughly enjoyed their company when they hung out together. *I could get used to this,* Anna thought. She was grateful they found each other again. And she was content with being in love without any of the prior reservations.

"Mom," Ashleigh said on the way out. "I think I'm okay with staying with you and Grandma in Magnolia Hill now. I like it here."

Anna did a double take. "Say that again? I don't think I heard you right."

Ashleigh blushed. "I like it here."

Anna had hoped that one day Ashleigh would come around. That it was only a couple of months after the move was a miracle. She rushed over to her daughter and almost knocked her over hugging her and kissing her on her forehead. She couldn't help it.

"Ew, Mom! Okay already! Too much!"

Anna backed off. "Sorry, but you don't know how happy this makes me."

"Well, the only thing that could make me even happier"—Ashleigh paused for impact—"would be if Sarah and I could be sisters."

"Would it, now?" Jason teased.

"Just think about it, Dad," Sarah said, holding the screen door open for her

Ashleigh. "We'll go to the movies now so you can talk."

"You girls already did your part. The rest is up to us," Jason said. "Now go and have fun at the theater."

They watched the kids walk down the driveway to wait on Sean to pick them up.

"Oh, I miss the drive-in," Anna said, her heart filling with nostalgia.

He coughed a little. "Remember, most of the time we didn't even pay attention to the movie. We were too busy..."

"What are ya'll talkin' about?" Maggie asked as she joined them, her face glowing.

"Nothing," Anna said. "We should ask what took you so long on the phone. You've been talking for hours. It can't be Mrs. Wilson. You don't have a secret admirer, do you?"

"If you must know, honey, it was your dad."

Anna was flabbergasted and didn't know how to respond to the news. Her mom looked happy, so it couldn't have gone that badly.

"Let's have a seat," Maggie said.

They walked over to the kitchen table, and Jason pulled a chair out for Maggie to sit.

"Okay, continue..." Anna said, leaning forward. She didn't want to miss a word of what her mom was about to tell her about her dad.

"Well, we talked. He wanted to make sure we were okay. Your dad got a call a few days ago from a female reporter from Magnolia Hill Times who asked him a bunch of questions about me."

"Miriam Sue Webster," Jason and Anna said in unison.

"Anyway, she tried to grill him with questions about our family. Rafael said he didn't give her anything to work with, but he knew that something wasn't right and was worried sick about us."

"Mom, I gotta ask," Anna said. "Did he take money from Grandpa to leave you?"

Maggie nodded, but before Anna could get upset, she continued. "This is what he told me: As you know, Rafael came from Puerto Rico. You should know that your grandpa always wanted the best for me." She pulled her chair closer to the table and rested her elbows on it. "One day, after my pregnancy with you was showing, Rafael said that your grandpa stopped by the diner he worked at as a cook and asked for him. Rafael took his break, and they sat down for a talk. Your grandpa explained to him that if he loved me, he should go back to Puerto Rico and handed him a check to start a new life there."

Anna gasped. "Grandpa did?" She couldn't believe it. Not her grandpa.

"At first, Rafael was angry with him, but Grandpa told him he couldn't possibly afford to raise a baby with a diner job. He then convinced him that the baby would be better off raised in the Weaver family."

"He believed that?" Jason asked.

"Rafael's parents were very poor, and he knew my dad was right. As much as it hurt him, he took the money and moved down to Florida."

Anna shook her head. "How could he?"

Maggie smiled. "He hasn't spent a penny of that money, sweetie. He put it all in the bank. Later, he started adding some money from each paycheck he received to it. He wasn't sure he was ever going to see you, or even if you wanted to, but he was hopeful there would be an opportunity to give it to you."

"Oh?"

"In other words, he wanted me to tell you that you have close to five hundred thousand dollars in your account."

Anna about fell out of her chair. "No way!"

"He said, if you were okay with it, that he'd like to come up and see us."

"I don't know what to say, Mom."

Jason put his arm over her shoulder and squeezed. "Give him a chance.

Not for the money but to see you. See what happens."

"Anna," Maggie said, "we were very young then, and yes, it broke my heart when he left, but look at you—you did great. Maybe it was the right choice, not an ethical one on my dad's side, but maybe it was for the best."

"How can you say that, Mom?" she said, close to tears. "I always wanted a dad. I never had one, and you can forgive him that easy?"

"Trust me, it's not easy for me. I loved him, honey, more than anything, just like I love you. Also, the good book tells us to forgive."

"Can't argue with the Bible, Anna," Jason said and gave her a kiss on the forehead.

She had to admit, even though she had mixed feelings about her dad at the moment, she had a ton of questions to ask. Did she have brothers or sisters? What was he doing now? Did he marry? "Okay, I can't make any promises, but if it makes you happy, go ahead and invite him."

Exhausted from her night shift, Anna entered the front door of Maggie's house, dropped her lunch bag on the kitchen table, and contemplated sitting on one of the chairs but decided against it. If she relaxed now, she'd never make it up to her bed.

Her phone buzzed in her uniform cargo pocket. *Good morning, sunshine*, Jason's message read. *Ready for a good day's sleep?*

I'm about to pass out, she typed, stifling a yawn.

Let's go watch the football game tonight. Ashleigh and Sarah want to go, and I think we're taking Grady, too.

Stranger things had happened than getting Ashleigh to a football game under any other circumstances than duress, but her new friends were a wonderful influence in converting her city-mindset to one of actually enjoying a southern small-town life.

I'd love to, Anna replied. She hadn't seen a local football game in ages.

Good, I'll pick you up around six. Now get some sleep! Love you.

She smiled. *Love you, too.*

Later that evening, Jason led her and the kids toward the bottom of the bleachers. The first two rows were reserved. To her surprise, Maggie, Mrs.

Wilson, and Jenna already took up some of the space.

"Is that for us?" Anna asked. "Who did you have to bribe for that? And how much did you have to shell out?"

"I know a man, who knows a man…" Jason chuckled. "Well, I can't take all the credit. Sean helped with this part."

"Wow, you two have a lot of influence in this town."

"I think Sean's badge carries more weight than my TV celebrity status," he admitted.

Sean arrived just a few minutes later in uniform, then disappeared again. Even more suspicious, while Jason had to go to the bathroom, Maggie insisted on getting refreshments with the kids while Dotty and Jenna went down to the sidelines to talk to Coach, leaving her by herself.

Anna twiddled her thumbs, then tested her breath and smelled her arm pits, just to make sure it wasn't her fault why everyone scattered.

"Hey," a familiar voice said behind her, and an ice cold shiver ran down her spine.

She turned around. "Grace."

Something was different. For the first time in her life, she saw her worst enemy at a loss for words. Grace didn't make eye contact at first and looked extremely uncomfortable. She tucked her hands in her jeans pockets.

Anna waited as Grace struggled to speak. When the awkwardness became too intense, Anna had to say something to break the ice. "What's up?" What's up? Was that all she could think of? Apparently, it was.

"I..." She hesitated. "I wanted to let you know that I told my boyfriend to go to hell that night you came by the house."

"Oh?"

"I also wanted to say I'm sorry for, you know, all the messed-up stuff I've done to you, and, well, the things I said about your family."

Anna was certain that she was dreaming, because Grace would never apologize to her in real life. Ever. Who was this woman eating crow in front of her? "Are you okay?" was all she could think to say.

"Yeah," Grace said. "I've started going to church and joined a program there to stop drinking and stuff."

"Well, I'm happy for you," Anna said, still unable to believe the change in Grace. "Really, I mean it!"

"What does she want from you?" Jenna asked, walking up behind her, not hiding her distaste.

"It's okay," Anna said. "Grace, would you like to sit with us?"

Jenna's eyes looked like they would pop out of their sockets any moment. "What the…"

"Nah, I'm here with some new friends of mine. I just wanted to stop by and talk to you, you know? Thanks for hearing me out." With that, Grace turned and gave a quick wave as she walked off.

"No way! What was that all about?" Jenna asked.

Anna saw Maggie and the kids come back to the bleachers loaded with food and drinks. Sean carried two cushioned folding stadium chairs for

Mrs. Wilson and Maggie. "I'll tell you later."

"Mom, let me help you with that." Anna took her burger, the nachos, and a drink and sat them on the bleachers, then saw her mom's two cheeseburgers. "Are those yours? You're not supposed to eat all that bread-y stuff with your diabetes."

"I'll toss the buns, and the tea is unsweetened. It tastes like crap, mind you."

"You'll get used to it, and the carb withdrawals should ease up in a couple of days."

"I hope so. That young doc who took over Doc Porter's practice is not cutting me any slack. No sugar, no starches. What's left to eat?"

"Plenty. You can still have most of the veggies in your garden, and you can have any meat and fish you want. Besides, we want to keep you around for a long while, with your eyesight intact and all your fingers and toes attached. Besides, now that the yarn shop is hopping after the grand opening and Miriam Webster's surprisingly positive article in the paper, we still need you around for a good long while to keep it running."

"You don't need to be so dramatic about it." Maggie waved her off.

"I do, and you know it."

"So how come you still get to eat burgers with buns and nachos?"

Her mom had a point. Diabetes ran in her family, and if she kept eating the way she did, she'd be following right in her mother's footsteps. It was time for her to deal with her own food issues. No more excuses. "Fair enough." She grabbed one of the burgers and took the bun off. "I'm starting low-carb with you right now. We'll do this together. Doc will be proud of you."

"Speaking of the new doc..." They both stared at Jenna.

"Oh no!" Jenna shook her head violently and crossed her arms. "Over my dead body. He is rude, arrogant, and wants me out of business. Don't play these matchmaking games with me." She eyeballed the nachos. "Since you're now both on that low-carb diet, I'm sure you won't mind if I help myself to the nachos."

A few minutes later, there was some commotion on the football field but still no sign of Jason.

"What did ya'll do with Jason?" Anna asked.

Ashleigh took a bite of her burger. "Dunno," she said with her mouth full of food. "Maybe the game's about to start. It's about time, too. I'm getting bored."

Anna watched the JROTC Color Guard post the flags, and the Magnolia Hill High marching band play the national anthem.

Anna looked around again. Still no Jason. "Did he fall in, Mom?"

She laughed. "I doubt it. Chances are, he ran into some locals asking about the weather. I'm sure he'll be here any minute now."

The announcer said something about a special treat, when she saw Brandon walk out onto the football field with Jason. What in the world?

Sean, who was still in uniform, stood up from the bleachers and took Anna's hand. "Ma'am, you better come with me," he said and walked her out onto the field to join Jason.

Anna's head was spinning as realization dawned on her. Suddenly, the late summer heat seemed unbearable. She was sure that she was about to faint right in the middle of the football field.

Jason was holding a mic and reached for her hand with his free one. "Anna, we couldn't make it happen twenty years ago when we were seniors in Magnolia Hill High, but we found each other again. I figured, if a hurricane couldn't kill us"—Anna heard the audience laugh—"we are meant for each other."

Anna's heart raced, and her head made her feel like she was floating. She watched him dig in his front jean pocket, then get down on one knee.

"Anna Maria Weaver, will you finally marry me?"

Epilogue

Anna had been studying for hours when Jason snuck up from behind and kissed her on her head. He sat a small plate with a slice of low-carb chocolate cake from Jenna's shop on top of her book. "It's time to take a break, Mrs. Morrison."

She sighed. "What was I thinking going to med school? You should have talked me out of this crazy idea."

Jason laughed. "You always wanted to become a doctor, and now is your chance, especially since your education is pretty much paid for. Your dad is a really cool guy."

She had to agree. Anna had met him in person right after the engagement when he came up to see them. Maggie had not been the same since the visit, and they kept calling each other almost every day since then. Anna was endlessly happy for her.

The book in front of her was daunting. "I totally forgot how hard studying was." She leaned back in her chair and blew her bangs out of her face. "I used to know all of this stuff, but I've been out of school so long."

"But you're also acing every class, sweetheart, which is quite an accomplishment. Of course, I wouldn't expect any less from you. Remember, you were the smart one in school."

She stuck her tongue out at him, then contemplated the options in front of her: "Biochemistry, cake, or Jason," she said, thinking out loud. She pointed at each option, then tried a different order. "Cake. Chem. Jason." She paused. "Nope. This won't do." She then tried one more time. "Jason, cake, then biochem!" She tapped her index finger on her lips. "I think I'm happy with my prioritization."

Jason grinned. "So am I."

"Mom, where's the drill? Grady is hanging a small shelf in my room so I can put my trophy on it." She held up a silver plastic skateboard in her hand. "After that, Grady is helping Sarah and me to make more statement bracelets to sell at the shop. He has really good ideas."

"Are you ready for the next class on Wednesday evening?"

"We got a full roster again. We're trying to come up with new designs and other things we can teach." Ashleigh beamed.

"That's great," Jason said, but Anna knew he had other plans in mind than getting the tools out. "Sweetie, the drill is in the toolbox in the garage. Better yet, how about you three give your mom a break while she's studying? Go grab a burger and a soda at Mamaw's, which I hear is an awesome place to brainstorm things like designs and such."

Ashleigh grabbed the money from him and called up the stairs. "Hey Sarah, Grady! I've got some money, let's spend it on video games!"

Anna laughed as Jason shot her a glare.

Ashleigh smiled at him. "Thanks, and don't worry, Jason. We'll behave so you get some 'grown-up' time together."

"Ew," Sarah said, pinching her eyes closed.

"Money or not, I think we should go," Grady said. "I'm out of here."

"While we're out, we also should come up with some ideas for the big 'Don't Drink & Drive' campaign at school next month," Ashleigh suggested.

"Yes. Maybe we could print a lot of posters..." Sarah's voice trailed off as the teens left the house.

The front door slammed, and the teens were gone. Anna looked at Jason, and they both burst into laughter. "I think we're alone now..." Anna said, and they high-fived each other. Jason pulled her off the dining room chair.

"Wait," she said, then took a quick bite of the chocolate cake with icing.

Jason drew her close and kissed her on the lips. "Hmm, sweet."

Oh, how she loved this man. She finally found her true love...once again.

* * *

Hi there!

I hope you enjoyed reading Hurricane Beach.

How about a free bonus story?
If you haven't already, why not read my novella, FLOOD WATERS? It's exclusive to my Stormies (newsletter subscribers) and you can download it for free at https://bit.ly/2VDYUOb.

Wanna read on? Why don't you grab the 2nd book of the Southern Storms series? TWIST OF FATE is about Jenna and her cupcake bakery having to deal with the grumpy new doc in town. All I can say is that they don't like each other much and you're in for a treat...

You can purchase Twist of Fate at your favorite book retailer.

Book Club Questions

- Anna & Jason, once high school sweethearts, reunite in this novel while on an adventure of their lifetime.
  - Would you tag along to experience the power of a hurricane as it makes landfall, or would you prefer to watch it on TV from far, far away and the safety of your home?
  - If the latter, what if your

first love would ask you and you were both single?

- Do you think Ashleigh's reaction to being uprooted from her familiar life was typical for a teenager? Why or why not?
- Everyone knows a "Grace"— someone with a tough past who copes with their struggles by lashing out. Do you believe Grace's transformation through recovery will be long-lasting? What makes you think this?
- Several of the characters in this book are dealing with grief and guilt. Who did you emphasize with the most and why?
  - <u>Anna</u> - grieving the loss of a marriage she tried to save.

  - <u>Ashleigh</u> - struggling with the loss of her friends and the life she knew..
  - <u>Jason</u> - mourning his wife after a tragic accident.
  - <u>Sarah</u> - coping with the loss of her mother in a car crash.
- Hurricanes can be an exciting force of nature but yet so devastating. Do you think the novel described the experience realistically? Why or why not?
- What did you think about Jason and Anna's first kiss at Tybee Island? How did it make you feel?
- What was your absolute favorite part of the story?
- What did you think about the ending. Was it satisfying? Did you wish for more?

- Would you recommend this novel to a friend, another book club, or reading groups? Why or why not?

A printable copy of these questions and other book club resources can be downloaded at Lexie's website:

https://www.lexienicholas.com/bookclub/

Also by Lexie Nicholas

Southern Storms Series

Twist of Fate Book #2

Fire Watch Book #3

Christmas Blizzard Book #4

Flood Waters A free bonus novella exclusive to Lexie's mailing list subscribers. Never miss a new release. You can sign up here: https://bit.ly/2VDYUOb

***All books can be read as standalone stories.

Scan QR code with your
phone camera for more info.

About the Author

Besides her love for stormy weather, Lexie is also a huge fan of reading and writing sweet small town romance novels. Wanna smile a lot and cry a little? Lexie's got you covered!

She lives with her husband, their dog, and their two cats smack-dab in the middle of the beautiful state of Alabama. Although it gets hot and muggy in the summer, the beach and inspiration for fresh stories are only a weekend trip away.

Visit her at https://lexienicholas.com.

Want more? Lexie also writes sweet, lighthearted mystery romances as Nickie Cochran—think Hallmark-style love stories with a delightful ghostly twist.

Lexie loves to hear from her readers. You can find and follow her at these online places:

amazon.com/author/lexienicholas

facebook.com/LexieNicholasAuthor

instagram.com/lexienicholaswriter

bookbub.com/authors/lexie-nicholas

goodreads.com/Lexie_Nicholas